P9-CPX-355

He drew a great sobbing breath and threw the sword into the moon-drenched sea.

Incredibly it did not sink. It remained throbbing in the water and began to give off a howl of horrible malevolence.

Berkley Books by Michael Moorcock

THE CHRONICLES OF CORUM
ELRIC OF MELNIBONÉ
THE SAILOR ON THE SEAS OF FATE
THE WEIRD OF THE WHITE WOLF

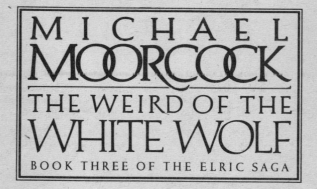

MICHAEL MOORCOCK
THE WEIRD OF THE WHITE WOLF
BOOK THREE OF THE ELRIC SAGA

BERKLEY BOOKS, NEW YORK

Part of this book originally appeared in a volume entitled *The Stealer of Souls*, published in the U.S.A. by Lancer Books in 1967. This edition contains two sections which appeared out of context in a collection entitled *The Singing Citadel* published in the U.S.A. by Berkley Medallion Books in 1970.

This Berkley Book contains the complete
text of the original edition.

THE WEIRD OF THE WHITE WOLF

A Berkley Book / published by arrangement with
the author

PRINTING HISTORY
DAW Books edition / March 1977
Berkley edition / September 1983

All rights reserved.
Copyright © 1967, 1970, 1977 by Michael Moorcock.
This book may not be reproduced in whole or in part,
by mimeograph or any other means, without permission.
For information address: The Berkley Publishing Group,
200 Madison Avenue, New York, New York 10016.

ISBN: 0-425-06289-9

A BERKLEY BOOK ® TM 757,375
The name "BERKLEY" and the stylized "B" with design
are trademarks belonging to Berkley Publishing Corporation.

PRINTED IN THE UNITED STATES OF AMERICA

THE WEIRD OF THE WHITE WOLF

To the memory of Ted Carnell, editor of
New Worlds and of *Science Fantasy*, who
published all the early Elric stories and
at whose suggestion I first began to write
the series. A kind and generous man who
gave me much encouragement in my
early years and without whom these
stories would never have been written.

THE WEIRD OF THE
WHITE WOLF
BOOK THREE OF THE ELRIC SAGA

Prologue

—◆—

THE DREAM OF EARL AUBEC

In which we learn something of how the Age of the Young Kingdoms emerged and of the part played by the Dark Lady, Myshella, whose fate would later be intertwined with that of Elric of Melnibone

. . .

From the glassless window of the stone tower it was possible to see the wide river winding off between loose, brown banks, through the heaped terrain of solid green copses which blended very gradually into the mass of the forest proper. And out of the forest, the cliff rose, grey and light-green, up and up, the rock darkening, lichen-covered, to merge with the lower, and even more massive, stones of the castle. It was the castle which dominated the countryside in three directions, drawing the eye from river, rock, or forest. Its walls were high and of thick granite, with towers; a dense field of towers, grouped so as to shadow one another.

Aubec of Malador marvelled and wondered how human builders could ever have constructed it, save by sorcery. Brooding and mysterious, the castle seemed to have a defiant air, for it stood on the very edge of the world.

At this moment the lowering sky cast a strange, deep-yellow light against the western sides of the towers, intensifying the blackness untouched by it. Huge billows of blue sky rent the general racing greyness above, and mounds of red cloud crept through to blend and produce more and subtler colourings. Yet, though the sky was impressive, it could not take the gaze away from the ponderous series of man-made crags that were Castle Kaneloon.

Earl Aubec of Malador did not turn from the window until it was completely dark outside; forest,

9

cliff, and castle but shadowy tones against the overall blackness. He passed a heavy, knotted hand over his almost bald scalp and thoughtfully went towards the heap of straw which was his intended bed.

The straw was piled in a niche created by a buttress and the outer wall and the room was well-lighted by Malador's lantern. But the air was cold as he lay down on the straw with his hand close to the two-handed broadsword of prodigious size. This was his only weapon. It looked as if it had been forged for a giant—Malador was virtually that himself—with its wide crosspiece and heavy, stone-encrusted hilt and five-foot blade, smooth and broad. Beside it was Malador's old, heavy armour, the casque balanced on top with its somewhat tattered black plumes waving slightly in a current of air from the window.

Malador slept.

His dreams, as usual, were turbulent; of mighty armies surging across the blazing landscapes, curling banners bearing the blazons of a hundred nations, forests of shining lance-tips, seas of tossing helmets, the brave, wild blasts of the war-horns, the clatter of hooves, and the songs and cries and shouts of soldiers. These were dreams of earlier times, of his youth when, for Queen Eloarde of Klant, he had conquered all the Southern nations—almost to the edge of the world. Only Kaneloon, on the very edge, had he not conquered, and this because no army would follow him there.

For one of so martial an appearance, these dreams were surprisingly unwelcome, and Malador woke several times that night, shaking his head in an attempt to rid himself of them.

He would rather have dreamed of Eloarde, though she was the cause of his restlessness, but he saw nothing of her in his sleep; nothing of her soft, black hair that billowed around her pale face, nothing of her green eyes and red lips and her proud, disdainful posture. Eloarde had assigned him to this quest and he had not gone willingly, though he had no choice, for as well as his mistress she was also his Queen. The Champion was traditionally her lover—and it was unthinkable to Earl Aubec that any other condition should exist. It was his place, as Champion of Klant, to obey and go forth from her palace to seek Castle Kaneloon alone and conquer it and declare it part of her Empire, so that it could be said Queen Eloarde's domain stretched from the Dragon Sea to World's Edge.

Nothing lay beyond World's Edge—nothing save the swirling stuff of unformed Chaos which stretched away from the Cliffs of Kaneloon for eternity, roiling and broiling, multicoloured, full of monstrous half-shapes—for Earth alone was Lawful and constituted of ordered matter, drifting in the sea of Chaos-stuff as it had done for aeons.

In the morning, Earl Aubec of Malador extinguished the lantern which he had allowed to remain alight, drew greaves and hauberk on to him, placed his black plumed helm upon his head, put his broadsword over his shoulder and sallied out of the stone tower which was all that remained whole of some ancient edifice.

His leathern-shod feet stumbled over stones that seemed partially dissolved, as if Chaos had once lapped here instead of against the towering Cliffs of Kaneloon. That, of course, was quite impossible, since Earth's boundaries were known to be constant.

Castle Kaneloon had seemed closer the night before and that, he now realised, was, because it was so huge. He followed the river, his feet sinking in the loamy soil, the great branches of the trees shading him from the increasingly hot sun as he made his

way towards the cliffs. Kaneloon was now out of
sight, high above him. Every so often he used his
sword as an axe to clear his way through the places
where the foliage was particularly thick.

He rested several times, drinking the cold water of
the river and mopping his face and head. He was
unhurried, he had no wish to visit Kaneloon, he
resented the interruption to his life with Eloarde
which he thought he had earned. Also he, too, had a
superstitious dread of the mysterious castle, which
was said to be inhabited only by one human occu-
pant—the Dark Lady, a sorceress without mercy who
commanded a legion of demons and other Chaos-crea-
tures.

He regarded the cliffs at midday and regarded the
path leading upward with a mixture of wariness and
relief. He had expected to have to scale the cliffs. He
was not one, however, to take a difficult route where
an easy one presented itself, so he looped a cord
around his sword and slung it over his back, since it
was too long and cumbersome to carry at his side.
Then, still in bad humour, he began to climb the
twisting path.

The lichen-covered rocks were evidently ancient,
contrary to the speculations of certain philosophers
who asked why Kaneloon had only been heard of a
few generations since. Malador believed in the general answer to this question—that explorers had
never ventured this far until fairly recently. He
glanced back down the path and saw the tops of the
trees below him, their foliage moving slightly in the
breeze. The tower in which he'd spent the night was
just visible in the distance and, beyond that, he
knew, there was no civilisation, no outpost of Man
for many days' journey North, East, or West—can
Chaos lay to the South? He had never been so close

to the edge of the world before and wondered how the sight of unformed matter would affect his brain.

At length he clambered to the top of the cliff and stood, arms akimbo, staring up at Castle Kaneloon which soared a mile away, its highest towers hidden in the clouds, its immense walls rooted on the rock and stretching away, limited on both sides only by the edge of the cliff. And, on the other side of the cliff, Malador watched the churning, leaping Chaos-substance, predominantly grey, blue, brown, and yellow at this moment, though its colours changed constantly, spew like the sea-spray a few feet from the castle.

He became filled with a feeling of such indescribable profundity that he could only remain in this position for a long while, completely overwhelmed by a sense of his own insignificance. It came to him, eventually, that if anyone did dwell in the Castle Kaneloon, then they must have a robust mind or else must be insane, and then he sighed and strode on towards his goal, noting that the ground was perfectly flat, without blemish, green, obsidian, and reflecting imperfectly the dancing Chaos-stuff from which he averted his eyes as much as he could.

Kaneloon had many entrances, all dark and unwelcoming, and had they all not been of regular size and shape they might have been so many cave-mouths.

Malador paused before choosing which to take, and then walked with outward purposefulness towards one. He went into blackness which appeared to stretch away forever. It was cold; it was empty and he was alone.

He was soon lost. His footsteps made no echo, which was unexpected; then the blackness began to give way to a series of angular outlines, like the walls of a twisting corridor—walls which did not reach the unsensed roof, but ended several yards above his head. It was a labyrinth, a maze. He paused and looked back and saw with horror that the maze wound off in many directions, though he was sure he had followed a straight path from the outside.

For an instant, his mind became diffused and madness threatened to engulf him, but he battened it down, unslung his sword, shivering. Which way? He pressed on, unable to tell, now, whether he went forward or backward.

The madness lurking in the depths of his brain filtered out and became fear and, immediately following the sensation of fear, came the shapes. Swift-moving shapes, darting from several different directions, gibbering, fiendish, utterly horrible.

One of these creatures kept at him and he struck at it with his blade. It fled, but seemed unwounded. Another came and another and he forgot his panic as he smote around him, driving them back until all had fled. He paused and leaned, panting, on his sword. Then, as he stared around him, the fear began to flood back into him and more creatures appeared—creatures with wide, blazing eyes and clutching talons, creatures with malevolent faces, mocking him, creatures with half-familiar faces, some recognisable as those of old friends and relatives, yet twisted into horrific parodies. He screamed and ran at them, whirling his huge sword, slashing, hacking at them, rushing past one group to turn a bend in the labyrinth and encounter another.

Malicious laughter coursed through the twisting corridors, following him and preceding him as he ran. He stumbled and fell against a wall. At first the wall seemed of solid stone, then, slowly it became soft and he sank through it, his body lying half in one corridor, half in another. He hauled himself through, still on hands and knees, looked up and saw Eloarde, but an Eloarde whose face grew old as he watched.

'*I am mad,*' he thought. '*Is this reality or fantasy—or both?*'

He reached out a hand, '*Eloarde!*'

She vanished but was replaced by a crowding horde of demons. He raised himself to his feet and flailed around him with his blade, but they skipped outside his range and he roared at them as he advanced. Momentarily, while he thus exerted himself, the fear left him again and, with the disappearance of the fear, so the visions vanished until he realised that the fear preceded the manifestations and he tried to control it.

He almost succeeded, forcing himself to relax, but it welled up again and the creatures bubbled out of the walls, their shrill voices full of malicious mirth.

This time he did not attack them with his sword, but stood his ground as calmly as he could and concentrated upon his own mental condition. As he did so, the creatures began to fade away and then the walls of the labyrinth dissolved and it seemed to him that he stood in a peaceful valley, calm and idyllic. Yet, hovering close to his consciousness, he seemed to see the walls of the labyrinth faintly outlined, and disgusting shapes moving here and there along the many passages.

He realised that the vision of the valley was as much an illusion as the labyrinth and, with this conclusion, both valley and labyrinth faded and he stood in the enormous hall of a castle which could only be Kaneloon.

The hall was unoccupied though well-furnished, and he could not see the source of the light, which was bright and even. He strode towards a table, on

which were heaped scrolls, and his feet made a satisfying echo. Several great metal-studded doors led off
from the hall, but for the moment he did not investigate them, intent on studying the scrolls and seeing
if they could help him unravel Kaneloon's mystery.

He propped his sword against the table and took
up the first scroll.

It was a beautiful thing of red vellum, but the
black letters upon it meant nothing to him and he
was astounded for, though dialects varied from place
to place, there was only one language in all the lands
of the Earth. Another scroll bore different symbols
still, and a third he unrolled carried a series of highly
stylised pictures which were repeated here and there
so that he guessed they formed some kind of alphabet.
Disgusted, he flung the scroll down, picked up his
sword, drew an immense breath, and shouted:

'Who dwells here? Let them know that Aubec,
Earl of Malador, Champion of Klant and Conqueror
of the South claims this castle in the name of Queen
Eloarde, Empress of all the Southlands!'

In shouting these familiar words, he felt somewhat
more comfortable, but he received no reply. He
lifted his casque a trifle and scratched his neck.
Then he picked up his sword, balanced it over his
shoulder, and made for the largest door.

Before he reached it, it sprang open and a huge,
manlike thing with hands like grappling irons
grinned at him.

He took a pace backward and then another until,
seeing that the thing did not advance, stood his
ground observing it.

It was a foot or so taller than he, with oval, multifaceted eyes that, by their nature, seemed blank. Its
face was angular and had a grey, metallic sheen.
Most of its body was comprised of burnished metal,
jointed in the manner of armour. Upon its head was

a tight-fitting hood, studded with brass. It had about
it an air of tremendous and insensate power, though
it did not move.

'A golem!' Malador exclaimed for it seemed to
him that he remembered such man-made creatures
from legends. 'What sorcery created *you*!'

The golem did not reply but its hands—which
were in reality comprised of four spikes of metal
apiece—began slowly to flex themselves; and still the
golem grinned.

This thing, Malador knew, did not have the same
amorphous quality of his earlier visions. This was
solid, this was real and strong, and even Malador's
manly strength, however much he exerted it, could
not defeat such a creature. Yet neither could he turn
away.

With a scream of metal joints, the golem entered
the hall and stretched its burnished hands towards
the earl.

Malador could attack or flee, and fleeing would be
senseless. He attacked.

His great sword clasped in both hands, he swung
it sideways at the golem's torso, which seemed to be
its weakest point. The golem lowered an arm and
the sword shuddered against metal with a mighty
clang that set the whole of Malador's body quaking.
He stumbled backward. Remorselessly, the golem
followed him.

Malador looked back and searched the hall in the
hope of finding a weapon more powerful than his
sword, but saw only shields of an ornamental kind
upon the wall to his right. He turned and ran to the
wall, wrenching one of the shields from its place and
slipping it on to his arm. It was an oblong thing,
very light, and comprising several layers of cross-
grained wood. It was inadequate, but it made him

feel a trifle better as he whirled again to face the golem.

The golem advanced, and Malador thought he
noticed something familiar about it, just as the
demons of the labyrinth had seemed familiar, but
the impression was only vague. Kaneloon's weird sorcery was affecting his mind, he decided.

The creature raised the spikes on its right arm
and aimed a swift blow at Malador's head. He
avoided it, putting up his sword as protection. The
spikes clashed against the sword and then the left
arm pistoned forward, driving at Malador's stomach.
The shield stopped his blow, though the spikes
pierced it deeply. He yanked the buckler off the
spikes, slashing at the golem's leg-joints as he did so.

Still staring into the middle-distance, with apparently no real interest in Malador, the golem advanced like a blind man as the earl turned and leapt
on to the table, scattering the scrolls. Now he
brought his huge sword down upon the golem's
skull, and the brass studs sparked and the hood and
head beneath it was dented. The golem staggered
and then grasped the table, heaving it off the floor so
that Malador was forced to leap to the ground. This
time he made for the door and tugged at its latch-
ring, but the door would not open.

His sword was chipped and blunted. He put his
back to the door as the golem reached him and
brought its metal hand down on the top edge of the
shield. The shield shattered and a dreadful pain shot
up Malador's arm. He lunged at the golem, but he
was unused to handling the big sword in this manner
and the stroke was clumsy.

Malador knew that he was doomed. Force and
fighting skill were not enough against the golem's insensate strength. At the golem's next blow he swung
aside, but was caught by one of its spike-fingers

which ripped through his armour and drew blood, though at that moment he felt no pain.

He scrambled up, shaking away the grip and fragments of wood which remained of the shield, grasping his sword firmly.

'*The soulless demon has no weak spot,*' he thought, '*and since it has no true intelligence, it cannot be appealed to. What would a golem fear?*'

The answer was simple. The golem would only fear something as strong or stronger than itself.

He must use cunning.

He ran for the upturned table with the golem after him, leaped over the table and wheeled as the golem stumbled but did not, as he'd hoped, fall. However, the golem was slowed by its encounter, and Aubec took advantage of this to rush for the door through which the golem had entered. It opened. He was in a twisting corridor, darkly shadowed, not unlike the labyrinth he had first found in Kaneloon. The door closed, but he could find nothing to bar it with. He ran up the corridor as the golem tore the door open and came lumbering swiftly after him.

The corridor writhed about in all directions, and, though he could not always see the golem, he could hear it and had the sickening fear that he would turn a corner at some stage and run straight into it. He did not—but he came to a door and, upon opening it and passing through it, found himself again in the hall of Castle Kaneloon.

He almost welcomed this familiar sight as he heard the golem, its metal parts screeching, continue to come after him. He needed another shield, but the part of the hall in which he now found himself had no wall-shields—only a large, round mirror of bright, clear-polished metal. It would be too heavy to be much use, but he seized it, tugging it from its hook. It fell with a clang and he hauled it up, dragging it with him as he stumbled away from the golem which had emerged into the room once more.

Using the chains by which the mirror had hung, he gripped it before him and, as the golem's speed increased and the monster rushed upon him, he raised this makeshift shield.

The golem shrieked.

Malador was astounded. The monster stopped dead and cowered away from the mirror. Malador pushed it towards the golem and the thing turned its back and fled, with a metallic howl, through the door it had entered by.

Relieved and puzzled, Malador sat down on the floor and studied the mirror. There was certainly nothing magical about it, though its quality was good. He grinned and said aloud:

'The creature *is* afraid of something. It is afraid of itself!'

He threw back his head and laughed loudly in his relief. Then he frowned. 'Now to find the sorcerers who created him and take vengeance on them!' He pushed himself to his feet, twisted the chains of the mirror more securely about his arm and went to another door, concerned lest the golem complete its circuit of the maze and return through the door. This door would not budge, so he lifted his sword and hacked at the latch for a few moments until it gave. He strode into a well-lit passage with what appeared to be another room at its far end—the door open.

A musky scent came to his nostrils as he progressed along the passage—the scent that reminded him of Eloarde and the comforts of Klant.

When he reached the circular chamber, he saw that it was a bedroom—a woman's bedroom full of the perfume he had smelled in the passage. He controlled the direction his mind took, thought of loyalty and Klant, and went to another door which led off from the room. He lugged it open and discovered a stone staircase winding upward. This he mounted, passing windows that seemed glazed with emerald or ruby, beyond which shadow-shapes flickered so that he knew he was on the side of the castle overlooking Chaos.

The staircase seemed to lead up into a tower, and when he finally reached the small door at its top he was feeling out of breath and paused before entering. Then he pushed the door open and went in.

A huge window was set in one wall, a window of clear glass through which he could see the ominous stuff of Chaos leaping. A woman stood by this window as if awaiting him.

'You are indeed a champion, Earl Aubec,' said she with a smile that might have been ironic.

'How do you know my name?'

'No sorcery gave it me, Earl of Malador—you shouted it loudly enough when you first saw the hall in its true shape.'

'Was not *that*, then, sorcery,' he said ungraciously, 'the labyrinth, the demons—even the valley? Was not the golem made by sorcery? Is not this whole cursed castle of a sorcerous nature?'

She shrugged. 'Call it so if you'd rather not have the truth. Sorcery, in your mind at least, is a crude thing which only hints at the true powers existing in the universe.'

He did not reply, being somewhat impatient of such statements. He had learned, by observing the philosophers of Klant, that mysterious words often disguised commonplace things and ideas. Instead, he looked at her sulkily and over-frankly.

She was fair, with green-blue eyes and a light complexion. Her long robe was of a similar colour to her eyes. She was, in a secret sort of way, very beautiful

and, like all the denizens of Kaneloon he'd encoun-
tered, a trifle familiar.

'You recognise Kaneloon?' she asked.

He dismissed her question. 'Enough of this—take
me to the masters of this place!'

'There is none but me, Myshella the Dark Lady—
and I am the mistress.'

He was disappointed. 'Was it just to meet you that
I came through such perils?'

'It was—and greater perils even than you think,
Earl Aubec. Those were but the monsters of your
own imagination!'

'Taunt me not, lady.'

She laughed. 'I speak in good faith. The castle
creates its defences out of your own mind. It is a rare
man who can face and defeat his own imagination.
Such a one has not found me here for two hundred
years. All since have perished by fear—until now.'

She smiled at him. It was a warm smile.

'And what is the prize for so great a feat?' he said
gruffly.

She laughed again and gestured towards the window which looked out upon the edge of the world
and Chaos beyond. 'Out there nothing exists as yet.
If you venture into it, you will be confronted again
by creatures of your hidden fancy, for there is nothing else to behold.'

She gazed at him admiringly and he coughed in
his embarrassment. 'Once in a while,' she said, 'there
comes a man to Kaneloon who can withstand such an
ordeal. Then may the frontiers of the world be ex-
tended, for when a man stands against Chaos it must
recede and new lands spring into being!'

'So that is the fate you have in mind for me, sorceress!'

She glanced at him almost demurely. Her beauty
seemed to increase as he looked at her. He clutched

at the hilt of his sword, gripping it tight as she moved gracefully towards him and touched him, as if by accident. 'There is a reward for your courage.' She looked into his eyes and said no more of the reward, for it was clear what she offered. 'And after—do my bidding and go against Chaos.'

'Lady, know you not that ritual demands of Klant's Champion that he be the queen's faithful consort? I would not betray my word and trust!' He gave a hollow laugh. 'I came here to remove a menace to my queen's kingdom—not to be your lover and lackey!'

'There is no menace here.'

'That seems true . . .'

She stepped back as if appraising him anew. For her this was unprecedented—never before had her offer been refused. She rather liked this solid man who also combined courage and imagination in his character. It was incredible, she thought, how in a few centuries such traditions could grow up—traditions which could bind a man to a woman he probably did not even love. She looked at him as he stood there, his body rigid, his manner nervous.

'Forget Klant,' she said, 'think of the power you might have—the power of true creation!'

'Lady, I claim this castle for Klant. That is what I came to do and that is what I do now. If I leave here alive, I shall be judged the conqueror and you must comply.'

She hardly heard him. She was thinking of various plans to convince him that her cause was superior to his. Perhaps she could still seduce him? Or use some drug to bewitch him? No, he was too strong for either, she must think of some other stratagem.

She felt her breasts heaving involuntarily as she looked at him. She would have preferred to have seduced him. It had always been as much her reward as the heroes who had earlier won over the dangers of Kaneloon. And then, she thought, she knew what to say.

'Think, Earl Aubec,' she whispered. 'Think—new lands for your queen's Empire!'

He frowned.

'Why not extend the Empire's boundaries farther?' she continued. 'Why not *make* new territories?'

She watched him anxiously as he took off his helm and scratched his heavy, bald head. 'You have made a point at last,' he said dubiously.

'Think of the honours you would receive in Klant if you succeeded in winning not merely Kaneloon— but that which lies *beyond*!'

Now he rubbed is chin. 'Aye,' he said, 'Aye ...' His great brows frowned deeply.

'New plains, new mountains, new seas—new populations, even—whole cities full of people fresh-sprung and yet with the memory of generations of ancestors behind them! All this can be done by *you*, Earl of Malador—for Queen Eloarde and Lormyr!'

He smiled faintly, his imagination fired at last. 'Aye! If I can defeat such dangers here—then I can do the same out there! It will be the greatest adventure in history! My name will become a legend— Malador, Master of Chaos!'

She gave him a tender look, though she had half-cheated him.

He swung his sword up on to his shoulder. 'I'll try this, lady.'

She and he stood together at the window, watching the Chaos-stuff whispering and rolling for eternity before them. To her it had never been wholly familiar, for it changed all the time. Now its tossing colours were predominantly red and black. Tendrils of mauve and orange spiralled out of this and writhed away.

Weird shapes flitted about in it; their outlines never clear, never quite recognisable.

He said to her: 'The Lords of Chaos rule this territory. What will they have to say?'

'They can say nothing, do little. Even they have to obey the Law of the Cosmic Balance which ordains that if man can stand against Chaos, then it shall be his to order and make Lawful. Thus the Earth grows, slowly.'

'How do I enter it?'

She took the opportunity to grasp his heavily muscled arm and point through the window. 'See—there—a causeway leads down from this tower to the cliff.' She glanced at him sharply. 'Do you see it?'

'Ah—yes—I had not, but now I do. Yes, a causeway.'

Standing behind him, she smiled a little to herself. 'I will remove the barrier,' she said.

He straightened his helm on his head. 'For Klant and Eloarde and only those do I embark upon this adventure.'

She moved towards the wall and raised the window. He did not look at her as he strode down the causeway into the multicoloured mist.

As she watched him disappear, she smiled to herself. How easy it was to beguile the strongest man by pretending to go his way! He might add lands to his Empire, but he might find their populations unwilling to accept Eloarde as their Empress. In fact, if Aubec did his work well, then he would be creating more of a threat to Klant than ever Kaneloon had been.

Yet she admired him, she was attracted to him, perhaps, because he was not so accessible, a little more than she had been to that earlier hero who had claimed Aubec's own land from Chaos barely two hundred years before. Oh, he had been a man! But he, like most before him, had needed no other persuasion than the promise of her body.

Earl Aubec's weakness had lain in his strength, she thought. By now he had vanished into the heaving mists.

She felt a trifle sad that this time the execution of the task given her by the Lords of Law had not brought her the usual pleasure.

Yes perhaps, she thought, she felt a more subtle pleasure in his steadfastness and the means she had used to convince him.

For centuries had the Lords of Law entrusted her with Kaneloon and its secrets. But the progress was slow, for there were few heroes who could survive Kaneloon's dangers—few who could defeat self-created perils.

Yet, she decided with a slight smile on her lips, the task had its various rewards. She moved into another chamber to prepare for the transition of the castle to the new edge of the world.

Thus were the seeds sewn of the Age of the Young Kingdoms, the Age of Men, which was to produce the downfall of Melnibone.

Book One

THE DREAMING CITY

Which tells how Elric came back to
Imrryr, what he did there, and how, at
last, his weird fell upon him . . .

ONE

~~~~~~~~~~~~~~~

'What's the hour?' The black-bearded man wrenched off his gilded helmet and flung it from him, careless of where it fell. He drew off his leathern gauntlets and moved closer to the roaring fire, letting the heat soak into his frozen bones.

'Midnight is long past,' growled one of the other armoured men who gathered around the blaze. 'Are you still sure he'll come?'

'It's said that he's a man of his word, if that comforts you.'

It was a tall, pale-faced youth who spoke. His thin lips formed the words and spat them out maliciously. He grinned a wolf-grin and stared the new arrival in the eyes, mocking him.

The newcomer turned away with a shrug. 'That's so—for all your irony, Yaris. He'll come.' He spoke as a man does when he wishes to reassure himself.

There were six men, now, around the fire. The sixth was Smiorgan—Count Smiorgan Baldhead of the Purple Towns. He was a short, stocky man of fifty years with a scarred face partially covered with a thick, black growth of hair. His eyes smouldered morosely and his lumpy fingers plucked nervously at his rich-hilted longsword. His pate was hairless, giving him his name, and over his ornate, gilded armour hung a loose woollen cloak, dyed purple.

Smiorgan said thickly, 'He has no love for his

cousin. He has become bitter. Yyrkoon sits on the
Ruby Throne in his place and has proclaimed him
an outlaw and a traitor. Elric needs us if he would
take his throne and his bride back. We can trust him.'

'You're full of trust tonight, Count,' Yaris smiled
thinly, 'a rare thing to find in these troubled times. I
say this—' He paused and took a long breath, staring
at his comrades, summing them up. His gaze flicked
from lean-faced Dharmit of Jharkor to Fadan of Lormyr who pursed his podgy lips and looked into the
fire.

'Speak up, Yaris,' petulantly urged the patrician-
featured Vilmirian, Naclon. 'Let's hear what you
have to say, lad, if it's worth hearing.'

Yaris looked towards Jiku the dandy, who yawned
impolitely and scratched his long nose.

'Well!' Smiorgan was impatient. 'What d'you say,
Yaris?'

'I say that we should start now and waste no more
time waiting on Elric's pleasure! He's laughing at us
in some tavern a hundred miles from here—or else
plotting with the Dragon Princes to trap us. For
years we have planned this raid. We have little time
in which to strike—our fleet is too big, too noticeable. Even if Elric has not betrayed us, then spies
will soon be running eastwards to warn the Dragons
that there is a fleet massed against them. We stand to
win a fantastic fortune—to vanquish the greatest
merchant city in the world—to reap immeasurable
riches—or horrible death at the hands of the Dragon
Princes, if we wait overlong. Let's bide our time no
more and set sail before our prize hears of our plan
and brings up reinforcements!'

'You always were too ready to mistrust a man,
Yaris.' King Naclon of Vilmir spoke slowly, care-
fully—distastefully eyeing the taut-featured youth.
'We could not reach Imrryr without Elric's

knowledge of the maze-channels which lead to its secret ports. If Elric will not join us—then our endeavour will be fruitless—hopeless. We need him. We must wait for him—or else give up our plans and return to our homelands.'

'At least I'm willing to take a risk,' yelled Yaris, anger lancing from his slanting eyes. 'You're getting old—all of you. Treasures are not won by care and forethought but by swift slaying and reckless attack.'

'Fool!' Dharmit's voice rumbled around the fire-flooded hall. He laughed wearily. 'I spoke thus in my youth—and lost a fine fleet soon after. Cunning and Elric's knowledge will win us Imrryr—that and the mightiest fleet to sail the Sighing Sea since Melniboné's banners fluttered over all the nations of the Earth. Here we are—the most powerful Sea Lords in the world, masters, every one of us, of more than a hundred swift vessels. Our names are feared and famous—our fleets ravage the coasts of a score of lesser nations. We hold *power*!' He clenched his great fist and shook it in Yaris' face. His tone became more level and he smiled viciously, glaring at the youth and choosing his words with precision.

'But all this is worthless—meaningless—without the power which Elric has. That is the power of knowledge—of sorcery, if I must use the cursed word. His fathers knew of the maze which guards Imrryr from sea-attack. And his fathers passed that secret on to him. Imrryr, the Dreaming City, dreams in peace—and will continue to do so unless we have a guide to help us steer a course through the treacherous waterways which lead to her harbours. We *need* Elric—we know it, and he knows it. That's the truth!'

'Such confidence, gentlemen, is warming to the heart.' There was irony in the heavy voice which came from the entrance to the hall. The heads of the six Sea Lords jerked towards the doorway.

Yaris' confidence fled from him as he met the eyes of Elric of Melniboné. They were old eyes in a fine featured, youthful face. Crimson eyes which stared into eternity. Yaris shuddered, turned his back on Elric, preferring to look into the bright glare of the fire.

Elric smiled warmly as Count Smiorgan gripped his shoulder. There was a certain friendship between the two. He nodded condescendingly to the other four and walked with lithe grace towards the fire. Yaris stood aside and let him pass. Elric was tall, broad-shouldered and slim-hipped. He wore his long hair bunched and pinned at the nape of his neck and, for an obscure reason, affected the dress of a Southern barbarian. He had long, knee-length boots of soft doe-leather, a breastplate of strangely wrought silver, a jerkin of chequered blue and white linen, britches of scarlet wool and a cloak of rustling green velvet. At his hip rested his runesword of black iron— the feared Stormbringer, forged by ancient and alien sorcery.

His bizarre dress was tasteless and gaudy, and did not match his sensitive face and long-fingered, almost delicate hands, yet he flaunted it since it emphasised the fact that he did not belong in any company—that he was an outsider and an outcast. But, in reality, he had little need to wear such outlandish gear—for his eyes and skin were enough to mark him.

Elric, Last Lord of Melniboné, was a pure albino who drew his power from a secret and terrible source.

Smiorgan sighed. 'Well, Elric, when do we raid Imrryr?'

Elric shrugged. 'As soon as you like; I care not. Give me a little time in which to do certain things.'

'Tomorrow? Shall we sail tomorrow?' Yaris said

hesitantly, conscious of the strange power dormant in the man he had earlier accused of treachery.

Elric smiled, dismissing the youth's statement. 'Three days' time,' he said. 'Three—or more.'

'Three days! But Imrryr will be warned of our presence by then!' Fat, cautious Fadan spoke.

'I'll see that your fleet's not found,' Elric promised. 'I have to go to Imrryr first—and return.'

'You won't do the journey in three days—the fastest ship could not make it.' Smiorgan gaped.

'I'll be in the Dreaming City in less than a day,' Elric said softly, with finality.

Smiorgan shrugged. 'If you say so, I'll believe it—but why this necessity to visit the city ahead of the raid?'

'I have my own compunctions, Count Smiorgan. But worry not—I shan't betray you. I'll lead the raid myself, be sure of that.' His dead-white face was lighted eerily by the fire and his red eyes smouldered. One lean hand firmly gripped the hilt of his runesword and he appeared to breathe more heavily. 'Imrryr fell, in spirit, five hundred years ago—she will fall completely soon—for ever! I have a little debt to settle. This is my only reason for aiding you. As you know I have made only a few conditions—that you raze the city to the ground and a certain man and woman are not harmed. I refer to my cousin Yyrkoon and his sister Cymoril . . .'

Yaris' thin lips felt uncomfortably dry. Much of his blustering manner resulted from the early death of his father. The old sea-king had died—leaving young Yaris as the new ruler of his lands and his fleets. Yaris was not at all certain that he was capable of commanding such a vast kingdom—and tried to appear more confident than he actually felt. Now he said: 'How shall we hide the fleet, Lord Elric?'

The Melnibonéan acknowledged the question. 'I'll

hide it for you,' he promised. 'I go now to do this—but make sure all your men are off the ships first—will you see to it, Smiorgan?'

'Aye,' rumbled the stocky count.

He and Elric departed from the hall together, leaving five men behind; five men who sensed an air of icy doom hanging about the overheated hall.

'How could he hide such a mighty fleet when we, who know this fjord better than any, could find nowhere?' Dharmit of Jharkor said bewilderedly.

None answered him.

They waited, tensed and nervous, while the fire flickered and died untended. Eventually Smiorgan returned, stamping noisily on the boarded floor. There was a haunted haze of fear surrounding him; an almost tangible aura, and he was shivering, terribly. Tremendous, racking undulations swept up his body and his breath came short.

'Well? Did Elric hide the fleet—all at once? What did he do?' Dharmit spoke impatiently, choosing not to heed Smiorgan's ominous condition.

'He has hidden it.' That was all Smiorgan said, and his voice was thin, like that of a sick man, weak from fever.

Yaris went to the entrance and tried to stare beyond the fjord slopes where many campfires burned, tried to make out the outlines of ships' masts and rigging, but he could see nothing.

'The night mist's too thick,' he murmured, 'I can't tell whether our ships are anchored in the fjord or not.' Then he gasped involuntarily as a white face loomed out of the clinging fog. 'Greetings, Lord Elric,' he stuttered, noting the sweat on the Melnibonéan's strained features.

Elric staggered past him, into the hall. 'Wine,' he mumbled, 'I've done what's needed and it's cost me hard.'

Dharmit fetched a jug of strong Cadsandrian wine and with a shaking hand poured some into a carved wooden goblet. Wordlessly he passed the cup to Elric who quickly drained it. 'Now I will sleep,' he said, stretching himself into a chair and wrapping his green cloak around him. He closed his disconcerting crimson eyes and fell into a slumber born of utter weariness.

Fadan scurried to the door, closed it and pulled the heavy iron bar down.

None of the six slept much that night and, in the morning, the door was unbarred and Elric was missing from the chair. When they went outside, the mist was so heavy that they soon lost sight of one another, though scarcely two feet separated any of them.

Elric stood with his legs astraddle on the shingle of the narrow beach. He looked back at the entrance to the fjord and saw, with satisfaction, that the mist was still thickening, though it lay only over the fjord itself, hiding the mighty fleet. Elsewhere, the weather was clear and overhead a pale winter sun shone sharply on the black rocks of the rugged cliffs which dominated the coastline. Ahead of him the sea rose and fell monotonously, like the chest of a sleeping water-giant, grey and pure, glinting in the cold sunlight. Elric fingered the raised runes on the hilt of his black broadsword and a steady north wind blew into the voluminous folds of his dark green cloak, swirling it around his tall, lean frame.

The albino felt fitter than he had done on the previous night when he had expended all his strength in conjuring the mist. He was well-versed in the art of nature-wizardry, but he did not have the reserves of power which the Sorcerer Emperors of Melniboné had possessed when they had ruled the world. His

ancestors had passed their knowledge down to him—
but not their mystic vitality and many of the spells
and secrets that he had were unusable, since he did
not have the reservoir of strength, either of soul or
of body, to work them. But for all that, Elric knew
of only one other man who matched his
knowledge—his cousin Yyrkoon. His hand gripped
the hilt tighter as he thought of the cousin who had
twice betrayed his trust, and he forced himself to
concentrate on his present task—the speaking of
spells to aid him on his voyage to the Isle of the
Dragon Masters whose only city, Imrryr the Beautiful, was the object of the Sea Lords' massing.

Drawn up on the beach, a tiny sailing-boat lay—Elric's own small ship, sturdy and far stronger, far
older, than it appeared. The brooding sea flung surf
around its timbers as the tide withdrew, and Elric realised that he had little time in which to work his
helpful sorcery.

His body tensed and he blanked his conscious
mind, summoning secrets from the dark depths of
his soul. Swaying, his eyes staring unseeingly, his
arms jerking out ahead of him and making unholy
signs in the air, he began to speak in a sibilant mon-
otone. Slowly the pitch of his voice rose, resembling
the scarcely heard shriek of a distant gale as it comes
closer—then, quite suddenly, the voice rose higher
until it was howling wildly to the skies and the air
began to tremble and quiver. Shadow-shapes began
slowly to form and they were never still but darted
around Elric's body as, stiff-legged, he started forward towards his boat.

His voice was inhuman as it howled insistently,
summoning the wind elementals—the *sylphs* of the
breeze; the *sharnahs*, makers of gales; the *h'Haar-
shanns*, builders of whirlwinds—hazy and formless,
they eddied around him as he summoned their aid

with the alien words of his forefathers who had, ages before, made unthinkable pacts with the elementals in order to procure their services.

Still stiff-limbed, Elric entered the boat and, like an automaton, his fingers ran up the sail and set it. Then a great wave erupted out of the placid sea, rising higher and higher until it towered over the vessel. With a surging crash, the water smashed down on the boat, lifted it and bore it out to sea. Sitting blank-eyed in the stern, Elric still crooned his hideous song of sorcery as the spirits of the air plucked at the sail and sent the boat flying over the water faster than any mortal ship could speed. And all the while, the deafening, unholy shriek of the released elementals filled the air about the boat as the shore vanished and open sea was all that was visible.

TWO

~~~~~~~~~~~~~~~

So it was, with wind-demons for shipmates, that Elric, last Prince of the Royal line of Melniboné, returned to the last city still ruled by his own race—the last city and the final remnant of Melnibonéan architecture. The cloudy pink and subtle yellow tints of her nearer towers came into sight within a few hours of Elric's leaving the fjord and just off-shore of the Isle of the Dragon Masters the elementals left the boat and fled back to their secret haunts among the peaks of the highest mountains in the world. Elric awoke, then, from his trance, and regarded with fresh wonder the beauty of his own city's delicate towers which were visible even so far away, guarded still by the formidable sea-wall with its great gate, the five-doored maze and the twisting, high-walled channels, of which only one led to the inner harbour of Imrryr.

Elric knew that he dare not risk entering the harbour by the maze, though he knew the route perfectly. He decided, instead, to land the boat further up the coast in a small inlet of which he had knowledge. With sure, capable hands, he guided the little craft towards the hidden inlet which was obscured by a growth of shrubs loaded with ghastly blue berries of a type decidedly poisonous to men since their juice first turned one blind and then slowly mad. This berry, the *nodoil*, grew only on Imrryr as did other rare and deadly plants.

Light, low-hanging cloud wisps streamed slowly across the sun-painted sky, like fine cobwebs caught by a sudden breeze. All the world seemed blue and gold and green and white, and Elric, pulling his boat up on the beach, breathed the clean, sharp air of winter and savoured the scent of decaying leaves and rotting undergrowth. Somewhere a bitch-fox barked her pleasure to her mate and Elric regretted the fact that his depleted race no longer appreciated natural beauty, preferring to stay close to their city and spend many of their days in drugged slumber. It was not the city which dreamed, but its overcivilised inhabitants. Elric, smelling the rich, clean winterscents, was wholly glad that he had his birthright and did not rule the city as he had been born to do.

Instead, Yyrkoon, his cousin, sprawled on the Ruby Throne of Imrryr the Beautiful and hated Elric because he knew that the albino, for all his disgust with crowns and rulership, was still the rightful King of the Dragon Isle and that he, Yyrkoon, was an usurper, not elected by Elric to the throne, as Melnibonéan tradition demanded.

But Elric had better reasons for hating his cousin. For those reasons the ancient capital would fall in all its magnificent splendour and the last fragment of a glorious Empire would be obliterated as the pink, the yellow, the purple and white towers crumbled—if Elric had his way and the Sea Lords were successful.

On foot, Elric strode inland, towards Imrryr, and as he covered the miles of soft turf, the sun cast an ochre pall over the land and sank, giving way to a dark and moonless night, brooding and full of evil portent.

At last he came to the city. It stood out in stark

black silhouette, a city of fantastic magnificence, in conception and in execution. It was the oldest city in the world, built by artists and conceived as a work of art rather than a functional dwelling place, but Elric knew that squalor lurked in many narrow streets and that the Lords of Imrryr left many of the towers empty and uninhabited rather than let the bastard population of the city dwell therein. There were few Dragon Masters left; few who would claim Melnibonéan blood.

Built to follow the shape of the ground, the city had an organic appearance, with winding lanes spiralling to the crest of the hill where stood the castle, tall and proud and many-spired, the final, crowning masterpiece of the ancient, forgotten artist who had built it. But there was no life-sound emanating from Imrryr the Beautiful, only a sense of soporific desolation. The city slept—and the Dragon Masters and their ladies and their special slaves dreamed drug-induced dreams of grandeur and incredible horror while the rest of the population, ordered by curfew, tossed on tawdry mattresses and tried not to dream at all.

Elric, his hand ever near his sword-hilt, slipped through an unguarded gate in the city wall and began to walk cautiously through the unlighted streets, moving upwards, through the winding lanes, towards Yyrkoon's great palace.

Wind sighed through the empty rooms of the Dragon towers and sometimes Elric would have to withdraw into places where the shadows were deeper when he heard the tramp of feet and a group of guards would pass, their duty being to see that the curfew was rigidly obeyed. Often he would hear wild laughter echoing from one of the towers, still ablaze with bright torchlight which flung strange, disturbing shadows on the walls; often, too, he would hear a chilling scream and a frenzied, idiot's yell as some wretch of a slave died in obscene agony to please his master.

Elric was not appalled by the sounds and the dim sights. He appreciated them. He was still a Melnibonéan—their rightful leader if he chose to regain his powers of kingship—and though he had an obscure urge to wander and sample the less sophisticated pleasures of the outside world, ten thousand years of a cruel, brilliant and malicious culture was behind him and the pulse of his ancestry beat strongly in his deficient veins.

Elric knocked impatiently upon the heavy, blackwood door. He had reached the palace and now stood by a small back entrance, glancing cautiously around him, for he knew that Yyrkoon had given the guards orders to slay him if he entered Imrryr.

A bolt squealed on the other side of the door and it moved silently inwards. A thin, seamed face confronted Elric.

'Is it the king?' whispered the man, peering out into the night. He was a tall, extremely thin individual with long, gnarled limbs which shifted awkwardly as he moved nearer, straining his beady eyes to get a glimpse of Elric.

'It's Prince Elric,' the albino said. 'But you forget, Tanglebones, my friend, that a new king sits on the Ruby Throne.'

Tanglebones shook his head and his sparse hair fell over his face. With a jerking movement he brushed it back and stood aside for Elric to enter. 'The Dragon Isle has but one king—and his name is Elric, whatever usurper would have it otherwise.'

Elric ignored this statement, but he smiled thinly and waited for the man to push the bolt back into place.

'She still sleeps, sire,' Tanglebones murmured as he climbed unlit stairs, Elric behind him.

'I guessed that,' Elric said. 'I do not underestimate my good cousin's powers of sorcery.'

Upwards, now, in silence, the two men climbed until at last they reached a corridor which was aflare with dancing torchlight. The marble walls reflected the flames and showed Elric, crouching with Tanglebones behind a pillar, that the room in which he was interested was guarded by a massive archer—a eunuch by the look of him—who was alert and wakeful. The man was hairless and fat, his blue-black gleaming armour tight on his flesh, but his fingers were curled around the string of his short, bone bow and there was a slim arrow resting on the string. Elric guessed that this man was one of the crack eunuch archers, a member of the Silent Guard, Imrryr's finest company of warriors.

Tanglebones, who had taught the young Elric the arts of fencing and archery, had known of the guard's presence and had prepared for it. Earlier he had placed a bow behind the pillar. Silently he picked it up and, bending it against his knee, strung it. He fitted an arrow to the string, aimed it at the right eye of the guard and let fly—just at the eunuch turned to face him. The shaft missed. It clattered against the man's gorget and fell harmlessly to the reed-strewn stones of the floor.

So Elric acted swiftly, leaping forward, his runesword drawn and its alien power surging through him. It howled in a searing arc of black steel and cut through the bone bow which the eunuch had hoped would deflect it. The guard was panting and his thick lips were wet as he drew breath to yell. As he opened his mouth, Elric saw what he had expected, the man was tongueless and was a mute. His own shortsword came out and he just managed to parry

Elric's next thrust. Sparks flew from the iron and
Stormbringer bit into the eunuch's finely edged
blade, he staggered and fell back before the nigro-
mantic sword which appeared to be endowed with a
life of its own. The clatter of metal echoed loudly
up and down the short corridor and Elric cursed the
fate which had made the man turn at the crucial moment. Grimly, swiftly, he broke down the eunuch's
clumsy guard.

The eunuch saw only a dim glimpse of his opponent behind the black, whirling blade which appeared to be so light and which was twice the length
of his own stabbing sword. He wondered, frenziedly,
who his attacker could be and he thought he recognised the face. Then a scarlet eruption obscured his
vision, he felt searing agony clutch at his face and
then, philosophically, for eunuchs are necessarily
given to a certain fatalism, he realised that he was to
die.

Elric stood over the eunuch's bloated body and
tugged his sword from the corpse's skull, wiping the
mixture of blood and brains on his late opponent's
cloak. Tanglebones had wisely vanished. Elric could
hear the clatter of sandalled feet rushing up the
stairs. He pushed the door open and entered the
room which was lit by two small candles placed at either end of a wide, richly tapestried bed. He went to
the bed and looked down at the raven-haired girl
who lay there.

Elric's mouth twitched and bright tears leapt into
his strange red eyes. He was trembling as he turned
back to the door, sheathed his sword and pulled the
bolts into place. He returned to the bedside and
knelt down beside the sleeping girl. Her features
were as delicate and of a similar mould as Elric's
own, but she had an added, exquisite beauty. She
was breathing shallowly, in a sleep induced not by

natural weariness but by her own brother's evil sorcery.

Elric reached out and tenderly took one fine-fingered hand in his. He put it to his lips and kissed it.

'Cymoril,' he murmured, and an agony of longing throbbed in that name. 'Cymoril—wake up.'

The girl did not stir, her breathing remained shallow and her eyes remained shut. Elric's white features twisted and his red eyes blazed as he shook in terrible and passionate rage. He gripped the hand, so limp and nerveless, like the hand of a corpse; gripped it until he had to stop himself for fear that he would crush the delicate fingers.

A shouting soldier began to beat at the door.

Elric replaced the hand on the girl's firm breast and stood up. He glanced uncomprehendingly at the door.

A sharper, colder voice interrupted the soldier's yelling.

'What is happening—has someone tried to see my poor sleeping sister?'

'Yyrkoon, the black hellspawn,' said Elric to himself.

Confused babblings from the soldier and Yyrkoon's voice raised as he shouted through the door. 'Whoever is in there—you will be destroyed a thousand times when you are caught. You cannot escape. If my good sister is harmed in any way—then you will never die, I promise you that. But you will pray to your Gods that you could!'

'Yyrkoon, you paltry rabble—you cannot threaten one who is your equal in the dark arts. It is I, Elric—your rightful master. Return to your rabbit hole before I call down every evil power upon, above, and under the Earth to blast you!'

Yyrkoon laughed hesitantly. 'So you have returned again to try to waken my sister. Any such attempt will not only slay her—it will send her soul into the deepest hell—where you may join it, willingly!'

By Arnara's six breasts—you it will be who samples the thousand deaths before long.'

'Enough of this.' Yyrkoon raised his voice. 'Soldiers—I command you to break this door down—and take that traitor alive. Elric—there are two things you will never again have—my sister's love and the Ruby Throne. Make what you can of the little time available to you, for soon you will be grovelling to me and praying for release from your soul's agony!'

Elric ignored Yyrkoon's threats and looked at the narrow window to the room. It was just large enough for a man's body to pass through. He bent down and kissed Cymoril upon the lips, then he went to the door and silently withdrew the bolts.

There came a crash as a soldier flung his weight against the door. It swung open, pitching the man forward to stumble and fall on his face. Elric drew his sword, lifted it high and chopped at the warrior's neck. The head sprang from its shoulders and Elric yelled loudly in a deep, rolling voice.

'*Arioch! Arioch!* I give you blood and souls—only aid me now! This man I give you, mighty King of Hell—aid your servant, Elric of Melniboné!'

Three soldiers entered the room in a bunch. Elric struck at one and sheared off half his face. The man screamed horribly.

'Arioch, Lord of the Darks—I give you blood and souls. Aid me, evil one!'

In the far corner of the gloomy room, a blacker mist began slowly, to form. But the soldiers pressed closer and Elric was hard put to hold them back.

He was screaming the name of Arioch, Lord of the Higher Hell, incessantly, almost unconsciously as he was pressed back further by the weight of the warriors' numbers. Behind them, Yyrkoon mouthed in

rage and frusttation, urging his men, still, to take Elric alive. This necessity gave Elric some small advantage—that and the runesword Stormbringer which
was glowing with a strange black luminousness and
the shrill howling it gave out was grating into the
ears of those who heard it. Two more corpses now
littered the carpeted floor of the chamber, their blood
soaking into the fine fabric.

'*Blood and souls for my lord Arioch!*'

The dark mist heaved and began to take shape,
Elric spared a look towards the corner and shuddered despite his inurement to hell-born horror.
The warriors now had their backs to the thing in the
corner and Elric was by the window. The amorphous mass that was a less than pleasant manifestation of Elric's fickle patron God, heaved again and
Elric made out its intolerably alien shape. Bile
flooded into his mouth and as he drove the soldiers
towards the thing which was sinuously flooding forward he fought against madness.

Suddenly, the soldiers seemed to sense that there
was something behind them. They turned, four of
them, and each screamed insanely as the black horror made one final rush to engulf them. Arioch
crouched over them, sucking out their souls. Then,
slowly, their bones began to give and snap and still
shrieking bestially the men flopped like obnoxious
invertebrates upon the floor; their spines broken,
they still lived. Elric turned away, thankful for once
that Cymoril slept, and leapt to the window ledge.
He looked down and realised with despair that he
was not going to escape by that route after all.
Several hundred feet lay between him and the ground.
He rushed to the door where Yyrkoon, his eyes wide
with fear, was trying to drive Arioch back. Arioch was
already fading.

Elric pushed past his cousin, spared a final glance

for Cymoril, then ran the way he had come, his feet slipping on blood. Tanglebones met him at the head of the dark stairway.

'What has happened, King Elric—what's in there?'

Elric seized Tanglebones by his lean shoulder and made him descend the stairs. 'No time,' he panted, 'but we must hurry while Yyrkoon is still engaged with his current problem. In five days' time Imrryr will experience a new phase in her history—perhaps the last. I want you to make sure that Cymoril is safe. Is that clear?'

'Aye, Lord, but . . .'

They reached the door and Tanglebones shot the bolts and opened it.

'There is no time for me to say anything else. I must escape while I can. I will return in five days— with companions. You will realise what I mean when that time comes. Take Cymoril to the Tower of D'a'rputna—and await me there.'

Then Elric was gone, soft-footed, running into the night with the shrieks of the dying still ringing through the blackness after him.

THREE

~~~~~~~~~~~~~~~~~~

Elric stood unspeaking in the prow of Count Smiorgan's flagship. Since his return to the fjord and the fleet's subsequent sailing for open sea, he had spoken only orders, and those in the tersest of terms. The Sea Lords muttered that a great hate lay in him, that it festered his soul and made him a dangerous man to have as comrade or enemy; and even Count Smiorgan avoided the moody albino.

The reaver prows struck eastward and the sea was black with light ships dancing on the bright water in all directions; they looked like the shadow of some enormous sea-bird flung on the water. Nearly half a thousand fighting ships stained the ocean—all of them of similar form, long and slim and built for speed rather than battle, since they were for coast-raiding and trading. Sails were caught by the pale sun; bright colours of fresh canvas—orange, blue, black, purple, red, yellow, light green or white. And every ship had sixteen or more rowers—each rower a fighting man. The crews of the ships were also the warriors who would attack Imrryr—there was no wastage of good man-power since the sea-nations were underpopulated, losing hundreds of men each year in their regular raids.

In the centre of the great fleet, certain larger vessels sailed. These carried great catapults on their decks and were to be used for storming the sea wall of Imrryr. Count Smiorgan and the other Lords looked at their ships with pride, but Elric only stared ahead of him, never sleeping, rarely moving, his white face lashed by salt spray and wind, his white hand tight upon his swordhilt.

The reaver ships ploughed steadily eastwards—forging towards the Dragon Isle and fantastic wealth—or hellish horror. Relentlessly, doom-driven, they beat onwards, their oars splashing in unison, their sails bellying taut with a good wind.

Onwards they sailed, towards Imrryr the Beautiful, to rape and plunder the world's oldest city.

Two days after the fleet had set sail, the coastline of the Dragon Isle was sighted and the rattle of arms replaced the sound of oars as the mighty fleet hove to and prepared to accomplish what sane men thought impossible.

Orders were bellowed from ship to ship and the fleet began to mass into battle formation, then the oars creaked in their grooves and ponderously, with sails now furled, the fleet moved forward again.

It was a clear day, cold and fresh, and there was a tense excitement about all the men, from Sea Lord to galley hand, as they considered the immediate future and what it might bring. Serpent prows bent towards the great stone wall which blocked off the first entrance to the harbour. It was nearly a hundred feet high and towers were built upon it—more functional than the lace-like spires of the city which shimmered in the distance, behind them. The ships of Imrryr were the only vessels allowed to pass through the great gate in the centre of the wall and the route through the maze—the exact entrance even—was a well-kept secret from outsiders.

On the sea wall, which now loomed tall above the fleet, amazed guards scrambled frantically to their posts. To them, threat of attack was well-nigh unthinkable, yet here it was—a great fleet, the greatest they had ever seen—come against Imrryr the Beautiful! They took to their posts, their yellow cloaks and kilts rustling, their bronze armour rattling, but they moved with bewildered reluctance as if refusing to accept what they saw. And they went to their posts with desperate fatalism, knowing that even if the ships never entered the maze itself, they would not be alive to witness the reavers' failure.

Dyvim Tarkan, Commander of the Wall, was a sensitive man who loved life and its pleasures. He was highbrowed and handsome, with a thin wisp of beard and a tiny moustache. He looked well in the bronze armour and high-plumed helmet; he did not want to die. He issued terse orders to his men and, with well-ordered precision, they obeyed him. He listened with concern to the distant shouts from the ships and he wondered what the first move of the reavers would be. He did not wait long for his answer.

A catapult on one of the leading vessels twanged throatily and its throwing arm rushed up, releasing a great rock which sailed, with every appearance of leisurely grace, towards the wall. It fell short and splashed into the sea which frothed against the stones of the wall.

Swallowing hard and trying to control the shake in his voice, Dyvim Tarkan ordered his own catapult to discharge. With a thudding crash the release rope was cut and a retaliatory iron ball went hurtling towards the enemy fleet. So tight-packed were the ships that the ball could not miss—it struck full on the deck of the flagship of Dharmit of Jharkor and crushed the timbers in. Within seconds, accompanied by the cries of maimed and drowning men, the ship had sunk and Dharmit with it. Some of the crew were taken aboard other vessels but the wounded were left to drown.

Another catapult sounded and this time a tower full of archers was squarely hit. Masonry erupted outwards and those who still lived fell sickeningly to die in the foam-tipped sea lashing the wall. This time, angered by the deaths of their comrades, Imrryrian archers sent back a stream of slim arrows into the enemy's midst. Reavers howled as red-fletched shafts buried themselves thirstily in flesh. But reavers returned the arrows liberally and soon only a handful of men were left on the wall as further catapult rocks smashed into towers and men, destroying their only war-machine and part of the wall besides.

Dyvim Tarkan still lived, though red blood stained his yellow tunic and an arrow shaft protruded from his left shoulder. He still lived when the first ram-ship moved intractably towards the great wooden gate and smashed against it, weakening it. A second ship sailed in beside it and, between them, they stove in the gate and glided through the entrance; the first non-Imrryrian ships ever to do such a thing. Perhaps it was outraged horror that tradition had been broken which caused poor Dyvim Tarkan to lose his footing at the edge of the wall and fall screaming down to break his neck on the deck of Count Smiorgan's flagship as it sailed triumphantly through the gate.

Now the ram-ships made way for Count Smiorgan's craft, for Elric had to lead the way through the maze. Ahead of them loomed five tall entrances, black gaping maws all alike in shape and size. Elric pointed to the third from the left and with short strokes the oarsmen began to paddle the ship into the dark mouth of the entrance. For some minutes, they sailed in darkness.

'Flares!' shouted Elric. 'Light the flares!'

Torches had already been prepared and these were now lighted. The men saw that they were in a vast tunnel hewn out of natural rock which twisted tortuously in all directions.

'Keep close,' Elric ordered and his voice was magnified a score of times in the echoing cavern. Torchlight blazed and Elric's face was a mask of shadow and frisking light as the torches threw up long tongues of flame to the bleak roof. Behind him, men could be heard muttering in awe and, as more craft entered the maze and lit their own torches, Elric could see some torches waver as their bearers trembled in superstitious fear. Elric felt some discomfort as he glanced through the flickering shadows and his eyes, caught by torchflare, gleamed feverbright.

With dreadful monotony, the oars splashed onwards as the tunnel widened and several more cavemouths came into sight. 'The middle entrance,' Elric ordered. The steersman in the stern nodded and guided the ship towards the entrance Elric had indicated. Apart from the muted murmur of some men and the splash of oars, there was a grim and ominous silence in the towering cavern.

Elric stared down at the cold, dark water and shuddered.

Eventually they moved once again into bright sunlight and the men looked upwards, marvelling at the height of the great walls above them. Upon those walls squatted more yellow-clad, bronze-armoured archers and as Count Smiorgan's vessel led the way out of the black caverns, the torches still burning in the cool winter air, arrows began to hurtle down into the narrow canyon, biting into throats and limbs.

'Faster!' howled Elric. 'Row faster—speed is our only weapon now!'

With frantic energy the oarsmen bent to their sweeps and the ships began to pick up speed even though Imrryrian arrows took heavy toll of the reaver crewmen. Now the high-walled channel ran straight and Elric saw the quays of Imrryr ahead of him.

'Faster! Faster! Our prize is in sight!'

Then, suddenly, the ship broke past the walls and was in the calm waters of the harbour, facing the warriors drawn up on the quay. The ship halted, waiting for reinforcements to plunge out of the channel and join them. When twenty ships were through, Elric gave the command to attack the quay and now Stormbringer howled from its scabbard. The flagship's port side thudded against the quay as arrows rained down upon it. Shafts whistled all around Elric but, miraculously, he was unscathed as he led a bunch of yelling reavers on to land. Imrryrian axe-men bunched forward and confronted the reavers, but it was plain that they had little spirit for the fight—they were too disconcerted by the course which events had taken.

Elric's black blade struck with frenzied force at the throat of the leading axe-man and sheared off his head. Howling demoniacally now that it had again tasted blood, the sword began to writhe in Elric's grasp, seeking fresh flesh in which to bite. There was a hard, grim smile on the albino's colourless lips and his eyes were narrowed as he struck without discrimination at the warriors.

He planned to leave the fighting to those he had led to Imrryr, for he had other things to do—and quickly. Behind the yellow-garbed soldiers, the tall towers of Imrryr rose, beautiful in their soft and scintillating colours of coral pink and powdery blue, of gold and pale yellow, white and subtle green. One such tower was Elric's objective—the tower of D'a'rputna where he had ordered Tanglebones to take Cymoril, knowing that in the confusion this would be possible.

Elric hacked a blood-drenched path through those who attempted to halt him and men fell back, screaming horribly as the runesword drank their souls.

Now Elric was past them, leaving them to the bright blades of the reavers who poured on to the quayside, and was running up through the twisting streets, his sword slaying anyone who attempted to stop him. Like a white-faced ghoul he was, his clothing tattered and bloody, his armour chipped and scratched, but he ran speedily over the cobble-stones of the twisting streets and came at last to the slender tower of hazy blue and soft gold—the Tower of D'a'rputna. Its door was open, showing that someone was inside, and Elric rushed through it and entered the large ground-floor chamber. No one greeted him.

'Tanglebones!' he yelled, his voice roaring loudly even in his own ears. 'Tanglebones—are you here?' He leapt up the stairs in great bounds, calling his servant's name. On the third floor he stopped suddenly, hearing a low groan from one of the rooms. 'Tanglebones—is that you?' Elric strode towards the room, hearing a strangled gasping. He pushed open the door and his stomach seemed to twist within him as he saw the old man lying upon the bare floor of the chamber, striving vainly to stop the flow of blood which gouted from a great wound in his side.

'What's happened man—where's Cymoril?'

Tanglebones' old face twisted in pain and grief. 'She—I—I brought her here, master, as you ordered. But—' he coughed and blood dribbled down his wizened chin, 'but—Prince Yyrkoon—he—he apprehended me—must have followed us here. He—struck me down and took Cymoril back with him—said she'd be—safe in the Tower of B'aal'nezbett. Master—I'm sorry . . .'

'So you should be,' Elric retorted savagely. Then his tone softened. 'Do not worry, old friend—I'll avenge you and myself. I can still reach Cymoril now I know where Yyrkoon has taken her. Thank you for trying, Tanglebones—may your long journey down the last river be uneventful.'

He turned abruptly on his heel and left the chamber, running down the stairs and out into the street again.

The Tower of B'aal'nezbett was the highest tower in the Royal Palace. Elric knew it well, for it was there that his ancestors had studied their dark sorceries and conducted frightful experiments. He shuddered as he thought what Yyrkoon might be doing to his own sister.

The streets of the city seemed hushed and strangely deserted, but Elric had no time to ponder why this should be so. Instead he dashed towards the palace, found the main gate unguarded and the main entrance to the building deserted. This too was unique, but it constituted luck for Elric as he made his way upwards, climbing familiar ways towards the topmost tower.

Finally, he reached a door of shimmering black crystal which had no bolt or handle to it. Frenziedly, Elric struck at the crystal with his sorcerous blade but the crystal appeared only to flow and re-form. His blows had no effect.

Elric racked his mind, seeking to remember the single alien word which would make the door open. He dared not put himself in the trance which would have, in time, brought the word to his lips, instead he had to dredge his subconscious and bring the

word forth. It was dangerous but there was little else
he could do. His whole frame trembled as his face
twisted and his brain began to shake. The word was
coming as his vocal chords jerked in his throat and
his chest heaved.

He coughed the word out and his whole mind and
body ached with the strain. Then he cried:

'I command thee—open!'

He knew that once the door opened, his cousin
would be aware of his presence, but he had to risk it.
The crystal expanded, pulsating and seething, and
then began to flow *out*. It flowed into nothingness,
into something beyond the physical universe, beyond
time. Elric breathed thankfully and passed into the
Tower of B'aal'nezbett. But now an eerie fire, chilling and mind-shattering, was licking around Elric as
he struggled up the steps towards the central chamber. There was a strange music surrounding him,
uncanny music which throbbed and sobbed and
pounded in his head.

Above him he saw a leering Yyrkoon, a black
runesword also in his hand, the mate of the one in
Elric's own grasp.

'Hellspawn!' Elric said thickly, weakly, 'I see you
have recovered Mournblade—well, test its powers
against its brother if you dare. I have come to
destroy you, cousin.'

Stormbringer was giving forth a peculiar moaning
sound which sighed over the shrieking, unearthly
music accompanying the licking, chilling fire. The
runesword writhed in Elric's fist and he had difficulty in controlling it. Summoning all his strength
he plunged up the last few steps and aimed a wild
blow at Yyrkoon. Beyond the eerie fire bubbled yel-
low-green lava, on all sides, above and beneath. The
two men were surrounded only by the misty fire and
the lava which lurked beyond it—they were outside

the Earth and facing one another for a final battle. The lava seethed and began to ooze inwards, dispersing the fire.

The two blades met and a terrible shrieking roar went up. Elric felt his whole arm go numb and it tingled sickeningly. Elric felt like a puppet. He was no longer his own master—the blade was deciding his actions for him. The blade, with Elric behind it, roared past its brother sword and cut a deep wound in Yyrkoon's left arm. He howled and his eyes widened in agony. Mournblade struck back at Stormbringer, catching Elric in the very place he had wounded his cousin. He sobbed in pain, but continued to move upwards, now wounding Yyrkoon in the right side with a blow strong enough to have killed any other man. Yyrkoon laughed then— laughed like a gibbering demon from the foulest depths of Hell. His sanity had broken at last and Elric now had the advantage. But the great sorcery which his cousin had conjured was still in evidence and Elric felt as if a giant had grasped him, was crushing him as he pressed his advantage, Yyrkoon's blood spouting from the wound and covering Elric, also. The lava was slowly withdrawing and now Elric saw the entrance to the central chamber. Behind his cousin another form moved. Elric gasped. Cymoril had awakened and, with horror on her face, was shrieking at him.

The sword still swung in a black arc, cutting down Yyrkoon's brother blade and breaking the usurper's guard.

'Elric!' cried Cymoril desperately. 'Save me—save me now, else we are doomed for eternity.'

Elric was puzzled by the girl's words. He could not understand the sense of them. Savagely he drove Yyrkoon upwards towards the chamber.

'Elric—put Stormbringer away. Sheath your sword or we shall part again.'

But even if he could have controlled the whistling blade, Elric would not have sheathed it. Hate dominated his being and he would sheathe it in his cousin's evil heart before he put it aside.

Cymoril was weeping, now, pleading with him. But Elric could do nothing. The drooling, idiot thing which had been Yyrkoon of Imrryr, turned at its sister's cries and stared leeringly at her. It cackled and reached out one shaking hand to seize the girl by her shoulder. She struggled to escape, but Yyrkoon still had his evil strength. Taking advantage of his opponent's distraction, Elric cut deep through his body, almost severing the trunk from the waist.

And yet, incredibly, Yyrkoon remained alive, drawing his vitality from the blade which still clashed against Elric's own rune-carved sword. With a final push he flung Cymoril forward and she died screaming on the point of Stormbringer.

Then Yyrkoon laughed one final cackling shriek and his black soul went howling down to hell.

The tower resumed its former proportions, all fire and lava gone. Elric was dazed—unable to marshal his thoughts. He looked down at the dead bodies of the brother and the sister. He saw them, at first, only as corpses—a man's and a woman's.

Then dark truth dawned on his clearing brain and he moaned in grief, like an animal. He had slain the girl he loved. The runesword fell from his grasp, stained by Cymoril's lifeblood, and clattered unheeded down the stairs. Sobbing now, Elric dropped beside the dead girl and lifted her in his arms.

'Cymoril,' he moaned, his whole body throbbing. 'Cymoril—I have slain you.'

FOUR

~~~~~~~~~~~~~~~~~~~~~~~~

Elric looked back at the roaring, crumbling, tumbling, flame-spewing ruins of Imrryr and drove his sweating oarsmen faster. The ship, sail still unfurled, bucked as a contrary current of wind caught it and Elric was forced to cling to the ship's side lest he be tossed overboard. He looked back at Imrryr and felt a tightness in his throat as he realised that he was truly rootless, now; a renegade and a woman-slayer, though involuntarily the latter. He had lost the only woman he had loved in his blind lust for revenge. Now it was finished—everything was finished. He could envisage no future, for his future had been bound up with his past and now, effectively, that past was flaming in ruins behind him. Dry sobs eddied in his chest and he gripped the ship's rail yet more firmly.

His mind reluctantly brooded on Cymoril. He had laid her corpse upon a couch and had set fire to the Tower. Then he had gone back to find the reavers successful, straggling back to their ships loaded with loot and girl-slaves, jubilantly firing the tall and beautiful buildings as they went.

He had caused to be destroyed the last tangible sign that the grandiose, magnificent Bright Empire had ever existed. He felt that most of himself was gone with it.

Elric looked back at Imrryr and suddenly a

greater sadness overwhelmed him as a tower, as delicate and as beautiful as fine lace, cracked and
toppled with flames leaping about it.

He had shattered the last great monument to the
earlier race—his own race. Men might have learned
again, one day, to build strong, slender towers like
those of Imrryr, but now the knowledge was dying
with the thundering chaos of the fall of the Dreaming City and the fast-diminishing race of Melniboné.

But what of the Dragon Masters? Neither they nor
their golden ships had met the attacking reavers—
only their foot-soldiers had been there to defend the
city. Had they hidden their ships in some secret
waterway and fled inland when the reavers overran
the city? They had put up too short a fight to be
truly beaten. It had been far too easy. Now that the
ships were retreating, were they planning some sudden retaliation? Elric felt that they might have such
a plan—perhaps a plan concerning dragons. He shuddered. He had told the others nothing of the beasts
which Melnibonéans had controlled for centuries.
Even now, someone might be unlocking the gates of
the underground Dragon Caves. He turned his mind
away from the unnerving prospect.

As the fleet headed towards open sea, Elric's eyes
were still looking sadly towards Imrryr as he paid
silent homage to the city of his forefathers and the
dead Cymoril. He felt hot bitterness sweep over him
again as the memory of her death upon his own
sword-point came sharply to him. He recalled her
warning, when he had left her to go adventuring in
the Young Kingdoms, that by putting Yyrkoon on
the Ruby Throne as Regent, by relinquishing his
power for a year, he doubled them both. He cursed
himself. Then a muttering, like a roll of distant
thunder, spread through the fleet and he wheeled

sharply, intent on discovering the cause of the consternation.

Thirty golden-sailed Melnibonéan battle barges
had appeared on both sides of the harbour, issuing
from two mouths of the maze. Elric realised that
they must have hidden in the other channels, waiting to attack the fleet when they returned, satiated
and depleted. Great war-galleys they were, the last
ships of Melniboné and the secret of their building
was unknown. They had a sense of age and slumber-
ing might about them as they rowed swiftly, each
with four or five banks of great sweeping oars, to en-
circle the raven ships.

Elric's fleet seemed to shrink before his eyes until
it seemed as though it were a bobbing collection of
wood-shavings against the towering splendour of the
shimmering battle barges. They were well-equipped
and fresh for a fight, whereas the weary reavers were
intensely battle-tired. There was only one way to save
a small part of the fleet, Elric knew. He would have
to conjure a witch-wind for sailpower. Most of the
flagships were around him and he now occupied that
of Yaris, for the youth had got himself wildly drunk
and had died by the knife of an Melnibonéan slave
wench. Next to Elric's ship was Count Smiorgan's
and the stocky Sea Lord was frowning, knowing full
well that he and his ships, for all their superior numbers, would not stand up to a sea-fight.

But the conjuring of winds great enough to move
many vessels was a dangerous thing, for it released
colossal power and the elementals who controlled
the winds were apt to turn upon the sorcerer himself
if he was not more than careful. But it was the only
chance, otherwise the rams which sent ripples from
the golden prows would smash the reaver ships to
driftwood.

Steeling himself, Elric began to speak the ancient

and terrible, many-vowelled names of the beings
who existed in the air. Again, he could not risk the
trance-state, for he had to watch for signs of the elementals turning upon him. He called to them in a
speech that was sometimes high like the cry of a gan-
net, sometimes rolling like the roar of shore-bound
surf, and the dim shapes of the Powers of the Wind
began to flit before his blurred gaze. His heart
throbbed horribly in his ribs and his legs felt weak.
He summoned all his strength and conjured a wind
which shrieked wildly and chaotically about him,
rocking even the huge Melnibonéan ships back and
forth. Then he directed the wind and sent it into the
sails of some forty of the reaver ships. Many he could
not save for they lay even outside his wide range.

But forty of the craft escaped the smashing rams
and, amidst the sound of howling wind and sun-
dered timbers, leapt on the waves, their masts creak-
ing as the wind cracked into their sails. Oars were
torn from the hands of the rowers, leaving a wake of
broken wood on the white salt trail which boiled behind each of the reaver ships.

Quite suddenly, they were beyond the slowly clos-
ing circle of Melnibonéan ships and careering madly
across the open sea, while all the crews sensed a dif-
ference in the air and caught glimpses of strange,
soft-shaped forms around them. There was a discom-
forting sense of evil about the beings which aided
them, an awesome alienness.

Smiorgan waved to Elric and grinned thankfully.

'We're safe, thanks to you, Elric!' he yelled across
the water. 'I knew you'd bring us luck!'

Elric ignored him.

Now the Dragon Lords, vengeance-bent, gave chase.
Almost as fast as the magic-aided reaver fleet were the
golden barges of Imrryr, and some reaver galleys,

whose masts cracked and split beneath the force of the wind driving them, were caught.

Elric saw mighty grappling hooks of dully gleaming metal swing out from the decks of the Imrryrian galleys and thud with a moan of wrenched timber into those of the fleet which lay broken and powerless behind him. Fire leapt from catapults upon the Dragon Lords' ships and careered towards many a fleeing reaver craft. Searing, foul-stinking flame hissed like lava across the decks and ate into planks like vitriol into paper. Men shrieked, beating vainly at brightly burning clothes, some leaping into water which would not extinguish the fire. Some sank beneath the sea and it was possible to trace their descent as, flaming even below the surface, men and ships fluttered to the bottom like blazing, tired moths.

Reaver decks, untouched by fire, ran red with reaver blood as the enraged Imrryrian warriors swung down the grappling ropes and dropped among the raiders, wielding great swords and battle-axes and wreaking terrible havoc amongst the sea-ravens. Imrryrian arrows and Imrryrian javelins swooped from the towering decks of Imrryrian galleys and tore into the panicky men on the smaller ships.

All this Elric saw as he and his vessels began slowly to overhaul the leading Imrryrian ship, flag-galley of Admiral Magum Colim, commander of the Melnibonéan fleet.

Now Elric spared a word for Count Smiorgan. 'We've outrun them!' he shouted above the howling wind to the next ship where Smiorgan stood staring wide-eyed at the sky. 'But keep your ships heading westwards or we're finished!'

But Smiorgan did not reply. He still looked skyward and there was horror in his eyes; in the eyes of a man who, before this, had never known the quivering bite of fear. Uneasily, Elric let his own eyes follow the gaze of Smiorgan. Then he saw them.

They were dragons, without doubt! The great reptiles were some miles away, but Elric knew the stamp of the huge flying beasts. The average wingspan of these near-extinct monsters was some thirty feet across. Their snake-like bodies, beginning in a narrow-snouted head and terminating in a dreadful whip of a tail, were forty feet long and although they did not breathe the legendary fire and smoke, Elric knew that their venom was combustible and could set fire to wood or fabric on contact.

Imrryrian warriors rode the dragon backs. Armed with long, spear-like goads, they blew strangely shaped horns which sang out curious notes over the turbulent sea and calm blue sky. Nearing the golden fleet, now half-a-league away, the leading dragon sailed down and circled towards the huge golden flag-galley, its wings making a sound like the crack of lightning as they beat through the air.

The grey-green, scaled monster hovered over the golden ship as it heaved in the white-foamed turbulent sea. Framed against the cloudless sky, the dragon was in sharp perspective and it was possible for Elric to get a clear view of it. The goad which the Dragon Master waved to Admiral Magum Colim was a long, slim spear upon which the strange pennant of black and yellow zig-zag lines was, even at this distance, noticeable. Elric recognised the insignia on the pennant.

Dyvim Tvar, friend of Elric's youth, Lord of the Dragon Caves, was leading his charges to claim vengeance for Imrryr the Beautiful.

Elric howled across the water to Smiorgan. 'These are your main danger, now. Do what you can to stave them off!' There was a rattle of iron as the men prepared, near-hopelessly, to repel the new menace.

Witch-wind would give little advantage over the fast-flying dragons. Now Dyvim Tvar had evidently conferred with Magum Colim and his goad lashed out at the dragon throat. The huge reptile jerked upwards and began to gain altitude. Eleven other dragons were behind it, joining it now.

With seeming slowness, the dragons began to beat relentlessly towards the reaver fleet as the crewmen prayed to their own Gods for a miracle.

They were doomed. There was no escaping the fact. Every reaver ship was doomed and the raid had been fruitless.

Elric could see the despair in the faces of the men as the masts of the reaver ships continued to bend under the strain of the shrieking witch-wind. They could do nothing, now, but die . . .

Elric fought to rid his mind of the swirling uncertainty which filled it. He drew his sword and felt the pulsating, evil power which lurked in rune-carved Stormbringer. But he hated that power now—for it had caused him to kill the only human he had cherished. He realised how much of his strength he owed to the black-iron sword of his fathers and how weak he might be without it. He was an albino and that meant that he lacked the vitality of a normal human being. Savagely, futilely, as the mist in his mind was replaced by red fear, he cursed the pretensions of revenge he had held, cursed the day when he had agreed to lead the raid on Imrryr and most of all he bitterly vilified dead Yrkoon and his twisted envy which had been the cause of the whole doom-ridden course of events.

But it was too late now for curses of any kind. The loud slapping of beating dragon wings filled the air and the monsters loomed over the fleeing reaver craft. He had to make some kind of decision—though he had no love for life, he refused to die by the hands of his own people. When he died, he promised himself, it would be by his own hand. He made his decision, hating himself.

He called off the witch-wind as the dragon venom seared down and struck the last ship in line.

He put all his powers into sending a stronger wind into the sails of his own boat while his bewildered comrades in the suddenly becalmed ships called over the water, inquiring desperately the reason for his act. Elric's ship was moving fast, now, and might just escape the dragons. He hoped so.

He deserted the man who had trusted him, Count Smiorgan, and watched as venom poured from the sky and engulfed him in blazing green and scarlet flame. Elric fled, keeping his mind from thoughts of the future, and sobbed aloud, that proud prince of ruins; and he cursed the malevolent Gods for the black day when idly, for their amusement, they had spawned men.

Behind him, the last reaver ships flared into sudden appalling brightness and, although half-thankful that they had escaped the fate of their comrades, the crew looked at Elric accusingly. He sobbed on, not heeding them, great griefs racking his soul.

A night later, off the coast of an island called Pan Tang, when the ship was safe from the dreadful recriminations of the Dragon Masters and their beasts, Elric stood brooding in the stern while the men eyed him with fear and hatred, muttering of betrayal and heartless cowardice. They appeared to have forgotten their own fear and subsequent safety.

Elric brooded, and he held the black runesword in his two hands. Stormbringer was more than an ordinary battle-blade, this he had known for years, but now he realised that it was possessed of more sentience than he had imagined. The frightful thing had used its wielder and had made Elric destroy Cymoril. Yet he was horribly dependent upon it; he realised this with soul-rending certainty. But he feared and resented the sword's power—hated it bitterly for the chaos it had wrought in his brain and spirit. In an agony of uncertainty he held the blade in his hands and forced himself to weigh the factors involved. Without the sinister sword, he would lose pride—perhaps even life—but he might know the soothing tranquillity of pure rest; with it he would have power and strength—but the sword would guide him into a doom-racked future. He would savour power—but never peace.

He drew a great, sobbing breath and, blind misgiving influencing him, threw the sword into the moon-drenched sea.

Incredibly, it did not sink. It did not even float on the water. It fell point forwards into the sea and *stuck* there, quivering as if it were embedded in timber. It remained throbbing in the water, six inches of its blade immersed, and began to give off a weird devil-scream—a howl of horrible malevolence.

With a choking curse Elric stretched out his slim, whitely gleaming hand, trying to recover the sentient hellblade. He stretched further, leaning far out over the rail. He could not grasp it—it lay some feet from him, still. Gasping, a sickening sense of defeat overwhelming him, he dropped over the side and plunged into the bone-chilling water, striking out with strained, grotesque strokes, towards the hovering sword. He was beaten—the sword had won.

He reached it and put his fingers around the hilt. At once it settled in his hand and Elric felt strength seep slowly back into his aching body. Then he realised that he and the sword were interdependent, for though he needed the blade, Stormbringer, parasitic, required a user—without a man to wield it, the blade was also powerless.

'We must be bound to one another then,' Elric murmured despairingly. 'Bound by hell-forged chains and fate-haunted circumstance. Well, then— let it be thus so—and men will have cause to tremble and flee when they hear the names of Elric of Melniboné and Stormbringer, his sword. We are two of a kind—produced by an age which has deserted us. Let us give this age *cause* to hate us!'

Strong again, Elric sheathed Stormbringer and the sword settled against his side; then, with powerful strokes, he began to swim towards the island while the men he left on the ship breathed with relief and speculated whether he would live or perish in the bleak waters of that strange and nameless sea ...

Book Two

WHILE THE GODS LAUGH

*I, while the gods laugh, the world's
vortex am;
Maelstrom of passions in that hidden
sea
Whose waves of all-time lap the coasts
of me,
And in small compass the dark waters
cram.*

Mervyn Peake, *Shapes and Sounds,*
1941.

ONE

~~~~~~~~~~~~~~~

One night, as Elric sat moodily drinking alone in a tavern, a wingless woman of Myyrrhn came gliding out of the storm and rested her lithe body against him.

Her face was thin and frail-boned, almost as white as Elric's own albino skin, and she wore flimsy pale-green robes which contrasted well with her dark red hair.

The tavern was ablaze with candle-flame and alive with droning argument and gusty laughter, but the words of the woman of Myyrrhn came clear and liquid, carrying over the zesty din.

'I have sought you twenty days,' she said to Elric who regarded her insolently through hooded crimson eyes and lazed in a high-backed chair; a silver wine-cup in his long-fingered right hand and his left on the pommel of his sorcerous runesword Stormbringer.

'Twenty days,' murmured the Melnibonéan softly, speaking as if to himself; deliberately rude. 'A long time for a beautiful and lonely woman to be wandering the world.' He opened his eyes a trifle wider and spoke to her directly: 'I am Elric of Melniboné, as you evidently know. I grant no favours and ask none. Bearing this in mind, tell me why you have sought me for twenty days.'

Equally, the woman replied, undaunted by the albino's supercilious tone. 'You are a bitter man, Elric; I know this also—and you are grief-haunted for reasons which are already legend. I ask you no favours—but bring you myself and a proposition. What do you desire most in the world?'

'Peace,' Elric told her simply. Then he smiled ironically and said: 'I am an evil man, lady, and my destiny is hell-doomed, but I am not unwise, nor unfair. Let me remind you a little of the truth. Call this legend if you prefer—I do not care.

'A woman died a year ago, on the blade of my trusty sword.' He patted the blade sharply and his eyes were suddenly hard and self-mocking. 'Since then I have courted no woman and desired none. Why should I break such secure habits? If asked, I grant you that I could speak poetry to you, and that you have a grace and beauty which moves me to interesting speculation, but I would not load any part of my dark burden upon one as exquisite as you. Any relationship between us, other than formal, would necessitate my unwilling shifting of part of that burden.' He paused for an instant and then said slowly: 'I should admit that I scream in my sleep sometimes and am often tortured by incommunicable self-loathing. Go while you can, lady, and forget Elric for he can bring only grief to your soul.'

With a quick movement he turned his gaze from her and lifted the silver wine-cup, draining it and replenishing it from a jug at his side.

'No,' said the wingless woman of Myyrrhn calmly, 'I will not. Come with me.'

She rose and gently took Elric's hand. Without knowing why, Elric allowed himself to be led from the tavern and out into the wild, rainless storm which howled around the Filkharian city of Raschil. A protective and cynical smile hovered about his mouth as she drew him towards the sea-lashed quay-

side where she told him her name. Shaarilla of the
Dancing Mist, wingless daughter of a dead necro-
mancer—a cripple in her own strange land, and an
outcast.

Elric felt uncomfortably drawn to this calm-eyed
woman who wasted few words. He felt a great surge
of emotion well within him; emotion he had never
thought to experience again, and he wanted to take
her finely moulded shoulders and press her slim
body to his. But he quelled the urge and studied her
marble delicacy and her wild hair which flowed in
the wind about her head.

Silence rested comfortably between them while
the chaotic wind howled mournfully over the sea.
Here, Elric could ignore the warm stink of the city
and he felt almost relaxed. At last, looking away
from him towards the swirling sea, her green robe
curling in the wind, she said: 'You have heard, of
course, of the Dead Gods' Book?'

Elric nodded. He was interested, despite the need
he felt to disassociate himself as much as possible
from his fellows. The mythical book was believed to
contain knowledge which could solve many problems
that had plagued men for centuries—it held a holy
and mighty wisdom which every sorcerer desired to
sample. But it was believed destroyed, hurled into
the sun when the Old Gods were dying in the cosmic
wastes which lay beyond the outer reaches of the so-
lar system. Another legend, apparently of later
origin, spoke vaguely of the dark ones who had interrupted the Book's sunward coursing and had
stolen it before it could be destroyed. Most scholars
discounted this legend, arguing that, by this time,
the book would have come to light if it did still exist.

Elric made himself speak flatly so that he ap-

peared to be disinterested when he answered Shaarilla. 'Why do you mention the Book?'

'I know that it exists,' Shaarilla replied intensely,
'and I know where it is. My father acquired the
knowledge just before he died. Myself—and the
book—you may have if you will help me get it.'

Could the secret of peace be contained in the
book? Elric wondered. Would he, if he found it, be
able to dispense with Stormbringer?

'If you want it so badly that you seek my help,' he
said eventually, 'why do you not wish to keep it?'

'Because I would be afraid to have such a thing
perpetually in my custody—it is not a book for a
woman to own, but you are possibly the last mighty
nigromancer left in the world and it is fitting that
you should have it. Besides, you might kill me to obtain it—I would never be safe with such a volume in
my hands. I need only one small part of its wisdom.'

'What is that?' Elric inquired, studying her patri-
cian beauty with a new pulse stirring within him.

Her mouth set and the lids fell over her eyes.
'When we have the book in our hands—then you will
have your answer. Not before.'

'This answer is good enough,' Elric remarked
quickly, seeing that he would gain no more information at that stage. 'And the answer appeals to me.'
Then, half before he realised it, he seized her shoulders in his slim, pale hands and pressed his colourless lips to her scarlet mouth.

Elric and Shaarilla rode westwards, towards the
Silent Land, across the lush plains of Shazaar where
their ship had berthed two days earlier. The border
country between Shazaar and the Silent Land was a
lonely stretch of territory, unoccupied even by
peasant dwellings; a no-man's land, though fertile
and rich in natural wealth. The inhabitants of Sha-

zaar had deliberately refrained from extending their borders further, for though the dwellers in the Silent Land rarely ventured beyond the Marshes of the Mist, the natural borderline between the two lands, the inhabitants of Shazaar held their unknown neighbours in almost superstitious fear.

The journey had been clean and swift, though ominous, with several persons who should have known nothing of their purpose warning the travellers of nearing danger. Elric brooded, recognising the signs of doom but choosing to ignore them and communicate nothing to Shaarilla who, for her part, seemed content with Elric's silence. They spoke little in the day and so saved their breath for the wild love-play of the night.

The thud of the two horses' hooves on the soft turf, the muted creak and clatter of Elric's harness and sword, were the only sounds to break the stillness of the clear winter day as the pair rode steadily, nearing the quaking, treacherous trails of the Marshes of the Mist.

One gloomy night, they reached the borders of the Silent Land, marked by the marsh, and they halted and made camp, pitching their silk tent on a hill overlooking the mist-shrouded wastes.

Banked like black pillows against the horizon, the clouds were ominous. The moon lurked behind them, sometimes piercing them sufficiently to send a pale tentative beam down on to the glistening marsh or its ragged, grassy frontiers. Once, a moonbeam glanced off silver, illuminating the dark silhouette of Elric, but, as if repelled by the sight of a living creature on that bleak hill, the moon once again slunk behind its cloud-shield, leaving Elric thinking deeply. Leaving Elric in the darkness he desired.

Thunder rumbled over distant mountains, sounding like the laughter of far-off Gods. Elric shivered, pulled his blue cloak more tightly about him, and continued to stare over the misted lowlands.

Shaarilla came to him soon, and she stood beside him, swathed in a thick woollen cloak which could not keep out all the damp chill in the air.

'The Silent Land,' she murmured. 'Are all the stories true, Elric? Did they teach you of it in old Melniboné?'

Elric frowned, annoyed that she had disturbed his thoughts. He turned abruptly to look at her, staring blankly through his crimson-irised eyes for a moment and then saying flatly:

'The inhabitants are unhuman and feared. This I know. Few men ventured into their territory, ever. None have returned, to my knowledge. Even in the days when Melniboné was a powerful Empire, this was one nation my ancestors never ruled—nor did they desire to do so. The denizens of the Silent Land are said to be a dying race, far more evil than my ancestors ever were, who enjoyed dominion over the Earth long before men gained any sort of power. They rarely venture beyond the confines of their territory, nowadays, encompassed as it is by marshland and mountains.'

Shaarilla laughed, then, with little humour. 'So they are unhuman are they, Elric? Then what of my people, who are related to them? What of me, Elric?'

'You're human enough for me,' replied Elric insouciantly, looking her in the eyes. She smiled.

'No compliment,' she said, 'but I'll take it for one—until your glib tongue finds a better.'

That night they slept restlessly and, as he had predicted, Elric screamed agonisingly in his turbulent, terror-filled sleep and he called a name which made Shaarilla's eyes fill with pain and jealousy. That name was Cymoril. Wide-eyed in his grim sleep, Elric seemed to be staring at the one he named, speaking other words in a sibilant language which made Shaarilla block her ears and shudder.

The next morning, as they broke camp, folding the rustling fabric of the yellow silk tent between them, Shaarilla avoided looking at Elric directly but later, since he made no move to speak, she asked him a question in a voice which shook somewhat.

It was a question which she needed to ask, but one which came hard to her lips. 'Why do you desire the Dead Gods' Book, Elric? What do you believe you will find in it?'

Elric shrugged, dismissing the question, but she repeated her words less slowly, with more insistence.

'Very well then,' he said eventually. 'But it is not easy to answer you in a few sentences. I desire, if you like, to know one of two things.'

'And what is that, Elric?'

The tall albino dropped the folded tent to the grass and sighed. His fingers played nervously with the pommel of his runesword. 'Can an ultimate God exist—or not? That is what I need to know, Shaarilla, if my life is to have any direction at all.

'The Lords of Law and Chaos now govern our lives. But is there some being greater than them?'

Shaarilla put a hand on Elric's arm. 'Why must you know?' she said.

'Despairingly, sometimes, I seek the comfort of a benign God, Shaarilla. My mind goes out, lying awake at night, searching through black barrenness for something—anything—which will take me to it, warm me, protect me, tell me that there is order in the chaotic tumble of the universe; that it is consistent, this precision of the planets, not simply a brief, bright spark of sanity in an eternity of malevolent anarchy.'

Elric sighed and his quiet tones were tinged with hopelessness. 'Without some confirmation of the order of things, my only comfort is to accept the anarchy. This way, I can revel in chaos and know, without fear, that we are all doomed from the start—that our brief existence is both meaningless and damned. I can accept then, that we are more than forsaken, because there was never anything there to forsake us. I have weighed the proof, Shaarilla, and must believe that anarchy prevails, in spite of all the laws which seemingly govern our actions, our sorcery, our logic. I see only chaos in the world. If the Book we seek tells me otherwise, then I shall gladly believe it. Until then, I will put my trust only in my sword and myself.'

Shaarilla stared at Elric strangely. 'Could not this philosophy of yours have been influenced by recent events in your past? Do you fear the consequences of your murder and treachery? Is it not more comforting for you to believe in deserts which are rarely just?'

Elric turned on her, crimson eyes blazing in anger, but even as he made to speak, the anger fled him and he dropped his eyes towards the ground, hooding them from her gaze.

'Perhaps,' he said lamely. 'I do not know. That is the only *real* truth, Shaarilla. *I do not know*.'

Shaarilla nodded, her face lit by an enigmatic sympathy; but Elric did not see the look she gave him, for his own eyes were full of crystal tears which flowed down his lean, white face and took his strength and will momentarily from him.

'I am a man possessed,' he groaned, 'and without this devil-blade I carry I would not be a man at all.'

TWO

They mounted their swift, black horses and spurred them with abandoned savagery down the hillside towards the Marsh, their cloaks whipping behind them as the wind caught them, lashing them high into the air. Both rode with set, hard faces, refusing to acknowledge the aching uncertainty which lurked within them.

And the horses' hooves had splashed into quaking bogland before they could halt.

Cursing, Elric tugged hard on his reins, pulling his horse back on to firm ground. Shaarilla, too, fought her own panicky stallion and guided the beast to the safety of the turf.

'How do we cross?' Elric asked her impatiently.

'There was a map—' Shaarilla began hesitantly.

'Where is it?'

'It—it was lost. I lost it. But I tried hard to memorise it. I think I'll be able to get us safely across.'

'How did you lose it—and why didn't you tell me of this before?' Elric stormed.

'I'm sorry, Elric—but for a whole day, just before I found you in that tavern, my memory was gone. Somehow, I lived through a day without knowing it—and when I awoke, the map was missing.'

Elric frowned. 'There is some force working against us, I am sure,' he muttered, 'but what it is, I do not know.' He raised his voice and said to her:

79

'Let us hope that your memory is not too faulty, now. These Marshes are infamous the world over, but by all accounts, only natural hazards wait for us.' He grimaced and put his fingers around the hilt of his runesword. 'Best go first, Shaarilla, but stay close. Lead the way.'

She nodded, dumbly, and turned her horse's head towards the north, galloping along the bank until she came to a place where a great, tapering rock loomed. Here, a grassy path, four feet or so across, led out into the misty marsh. They could only see a little distance ahead, because of the clinging mist, but it seemed that the trail remained firm for some way. Shaarilla walked her horse on to the path and jolted forward at a slow trot, Elric following immediately behind her.

Through the swirling, heavy mist which shone whitely, the horses moved hesitantly and their riders had to keep them on short, tight rein. The mist padded the marsh with silence and the gleaming, watery fens around them stank with foul putrescence. No animal scurried, no bird shrieked above them. Everywhere was a haunting, fear-laden silence which made both horses and riders uneasy.

With panic in their throats, Elric and Shaarilla rode on, deeper and deeper into the unnatural Marshes of the Mist, their eyes wary and even their nostrils quivering for scent of danger in the stinking morass.

Hours later, when the sun was long past its zenith, Shaarilla's horse reared, screaming and whinnying. She shouted for Elric, her exquisite features twisted in fear as she stared into the mist. He spurred his own bucking horse forwards and joined her.

Something moved, slowly, menacingly in the clinging whiteness. Elric's right hand whipped over to his left side and grasped the hilt of Stormbringer.

The blade shrieked out of its scabbard, a black
fire gleaming along its length and alien power flowing from it into Elric's arm and through his body. A
weird, unholy light leapt into Elric's crimson eyes
and his mouth was wrenched into a hideous grin as
he forced the frightened horse further into the
skulking mist.

'Arioch, Lord of the Seven Darks, be with me
now!' Elric yelled as he made out the shifting shape
ahead of him. It was white, like the mist, yet somehow *darker*. It stretched high above Elric's head. It
was nearly eight feet tall and almost as broad. But it
was still only an outline, seeming to have no face or
limbs—only movement: darting, malevolent movement! But Arioch, his patron god, chose not to hear.

Elric could feel his horse's great heart beating between his legs as the beast plunged forward under
its rider's iron control. Shaarilla was screaming something behind him, but he could not hear the words.
Elric hacked at the white shape, but his sword met
only mist and it howled angrily. The fear-crazed
horse would go no further and Elric was forced to
dismount.

'Keep hold of the steed,' he shouted behind him to
Shaarilla and moved on light feet towards the darting shape which hovered ahead of him, blocking his
path.

Now he could make out some of its saliencies.
Two eyes, the colour of thin, yellow wine, were set
high in the thing's body, though it had no separate
head. A mouthing, obscene slit, filled with fangs, lay
just beneath the eyes. It had no nose or ears that Elric could see. Four appendages sprang from its upper
parts and its lower body slithered along the ground,
unsupported by any limbs. Elric's eyes ached as he
looked at it. It was incredibly disgusting to behold
and its amorphous body gave off a stench of death

and decay. Fighting down his fear, the albino inched forward warily, his sword held high to parry any thrust the thing might make with its arms. Elric recognised it from a description in one of his grimoires. It was a Mist Giant—possibly the only Mist Giant, Bellbane. Even the wisest wizards were uncertain how many existed—one or many. It was a ghoul of the swamp-lands which fed off the souls and the blood of men and beasts. But the Marshes of this Mist were far to the east of Bellbane's reputed haunts.

Elric ceased to wonder why so few animals inhabited that stretch of the swamp. Overhead the sky was beginning to darken.

Stormbringer throbbed in Elric's grasp as he called the names of the ancient Demon-Gods of his people. The nauseous ghoul obviously recognised the names. For an instant, it wavered backwards. Elric made his legs move towards the thing. Now he saw that the ghoul was not white at all. But it had no colour to it that Elric could recognise. There was a suggestion of orangeness dashed with sickening greenish yellow, but he did not see the colours with his eyes—he only *sensed* the alien, unholy tinctures.

Then Elric rushed towards the thing, shouting the names which now had no meaning to his surface consciousness. 'Balaan—Marthim! Aesma! Alastor! Saebos! Verdelet! Nizilfhm! Haborym! Haborym of the Fires Which Destroy!' His whole mind was torn in two. Part of him wanted to run, to hide, but he had no control over the power which now gripped him and pushed him to meet the horror. His sword blade hacked and slashed at the shape. It was like trying to cut through water—sentient, pulsating water. But Stormbringer had effect. The whole shape of the ghoul quivered as if in dreadful pain. Elric felt himself plucked into the air and his vision went. He could see nothing—do nothing but hack and cut at the thing which now held him.

Sweat poured from him as, blindly, he fought on.

Pain which was hardly physical—a deeper, horrifying pain, filled his being as he howled now in agony and struck continually at the yielding bulk which embraced him and was pulling him slowly towards its gaping maw. He struggled and writhed in the obscene grasp of the thing. With powerful arms, it was holding him, almost lasciviously, drawing him closer as a rough lover would draw a girl. Even the mighty power intrinsic in the runesword did not seem enough to kill the monster. Though its efforts were somewhat weaker than earlier, it still drew Elric nearer to the gnashing, slavering mouth-slit.

Elric cried the names again, while Stormbringer danced and sang an evil song in his right hand. In agony, Elric writhed, praying, begging and promising, but still he was drawn inch by inch towards the grinning maw.

Savagely, grimly, he fought and again he screamed for Arioch. A mind touched his—sardonic, powerful, evil—and he knew Arioch responded at last! Almost imperceptibly, the Mist Giant weakened. Elric pressed his advantage and the knowledge that the ghoul was losing its strength gave him more power. Blindly, agony piercing every nerve of his body, he struck and struck.

Then, quite suddenly, he was falling.

He seemed to fall for hours, slowly, weightlessly until he landed upon a surface which yielded beneath him. He began to sink.

Far off, beyond time and space, he heard a distant voice calling to him. He did not want to hear it; he was content to lie where he was as the cold, comforting stuff in which he lay dragged him slowly into itself.

Then some sixth sense made him realise that it
was Shaarilla's voice calling him and he forced himself to make sense out of her words.

'Elric—the marsh! You're in the marsh. Don't
move!'

He smiled to himself. Why should he move?
Down he was sinking, slowly, calmly—down into the
welcoming marsh . . . *Had there been another time
like this; another marsh?*

With a mental jolt, full awareness of the situation
came back to him and he jerked his eyes open.
Above him was mist. To one side a pool of unnam-
able colouring was slowly evaporating, giving off a
foul odour. On the other side he could just make
out a human form, gesticulating wildly. Beyond the
human form were the barely discernible shapes of
two horses. Shaarilla was there. Beneath him—

Beneath him was the marsh.

Thick, stinking slime was sucking him downwards
as he lay spread-eagled upon it, half-submerged already. Stormbringer was still in his right hand. He
could just see it if he turned his head. Carefully, he
tried to lift the top half of his body from the sucking
morass. He succeeded, only to feel his legs sink
deeper. Sitting upright, he shouted to the girl.

'Shaarilla! Quickly—a rope!'

'There is no rope, Elric!' She was ripping off her
top garment, frantically tearing it into strips.

Still Elric sank, his feet finding no purchase
beneath them.

Shaarilla hastily knotted the strips of cloth. She
flung the makeshift rope inexpertly towards the sinking albino. It fell short. Fumbling in her haste, she
threw it again. This time his groping left hand
found it. The girl began to haul on the fabric. Elric
felt himself rise a little and then stop.

'It's no good, Elric—I haven't the strength.'

Cursing her, Elric shouted: 'The horse—tie it to the horse!'

She ran towards one of the horses and looped the cloth around the pommel of the saddle. Then she tugged at the beast's reins and began to walk it away.

Swiftly, Elric was dragged from the sucking bog and, still gripping Stormbringer was pulled to the inadequate safety of the strip of turf.

Gasping, he tried to stand, but found his legs incredibly weak beneath him. He rose, staggered, and fell. Shaarilla knelt down beside him.

'Are you hurt?'

Elric smiled in spite of his weakness. 'I don't think so.'

'It was dreadful. I couldn't see properly what was happening. You seemed to disappear and then—then you screamed that—that name!' She was trembling, her face pale and taut.

'What name?' Elric was genuinely puzzled. 'What name did I scream?'

She shook her head. 'It doesn't matter—but whatever it was—it saved you. You reappeared soon afterwards and fell into the marsh . . .'

Stormbringer's power was still flowing into the albino. He already felt stronger.

With an effort, he got up and stumbled unsteadily towards his horse.

'I'm sure that the Mist Giant does not usually haunt this marsh—it was sent here. By what—or whom—I don't know, but we must get to firmer ground while we can.'

Shaarilla said: 'Which way—back or forward?'

Elric frowned. 'Why, forward, of course. Why do you ask?'

She swallowed and shook her head. 'Let's hurry, then,' she said.

They mounted their horses and rode with little caution until the marsh and its cloak of mist was behind them.

Now the journey took on a new urgency as Elric realised that some force was attempting to put obstacles in their way. They rested little and savagely rode their powerful horses to a virtual standstill.

On the fifth day they were riding through barren, rocky country and a light rain was falling.

The hard ground was slippery so that they were forced to ride more slowly, huddled over the sodden necks of their horses, muffled in cloaks which only inadequately kept out the drizzling rain. They had ridden in silence for some time before they heard a ghastly cackling baying ahead of them and the rattle of hooves.

Elric motioned towards a large rock looming to their right. 'Shelter there,' he said. 'Something comes towards us—possibly more enemies. With luck, they'll pass us.' Shaarilla mutely obeyed him and together they waited as the hideous baying grew nearer.

'One rider—several other beasts,' Elric said, listening intently. 'The beasts either follow or pursue the rider.'

Then they were in sight—racing through the rain. A man frantically spurring an equally frightened horse—and behind him, the distance decreasing, a pack of what at first appeared to be dogs. But these were not dogs—they were half-dog and half-bird, with the lean, shaggy bodies and legs of dogs but possessing birdlike talons in place of paws and savagely curved beaks which snapped where muzzles should have been.

'The hunting dogs of the Dharzi!' gasped Shaarilla. 'I thought that they, like their masters, were long extinct!'

'I, also,' Elric said. 'What are they doing in these parts? There was never contact between the Dharzi and the dwellers of this Land.'

'Brought here—by *something*,' Shaarilla whispered. 'Those devil-dogs will scent us to be sure.'

Elric reached for his runesword. 'Then we can lose nothing by aiding their quarry,' he said, urging his mount forward. 'Wait here, Shaarilla.'

By this time, the devil-pack and the man they pursued were rushing past the sheltering rock, speeding down a narrow defile. Elric spurred his horse down the slope.

'Ho there!' he shouted to the frantic rider. 'Turn and stand, my friend—I'm here to aid you!'

His moaning runesword lifted high, Elric thundered towards the snapping, howling devil-dogs and his horse's hooves struck one with an impact which broke the unnatural beast's spine. There were some five or six of the weird dogs left. The rider turned his horse and drew a long sabre from a scabbard at his waist. He was a small man, with a broad ugly mouth. He grinned in relief.

'A lucky chance, this meeting, good master!'

This was all he had time to remark before two of the dogs were leaping at him and he was forced to give his whole attention to defending himself from their slashing talons and snapping beaks.

The other three dogs concentrated their vicious attention upon Elric. One leapt high, its beak aimed at Elric's throat. He felt foul breath on his face and hastily brought Stormbringer round in an arc which chopped the dog in two. Filthy blood spattered Elric and his horse and the scent of it seemed to increase the fury of the other dogs' attack. But the blood made the dancing black runesword sing an almost ecstatic tune and Elric felt it writhe in his grasp and stab at another of the hideous dogs. The point caught the beast just below its breastbone as it reared up at the albino. It screamed in terrible agony and turned its beak to seize the blade. As the beak connected with the lambent black metal of the sword, a foul stench, akin to the smell of burning, struck Elric's nostrils and the beast's scream broke off sharply.

Engaged with the remaining devil-dog, Elric caught a fleeting glimpse of the charred corpse. His horse was rearing high, lashing at the last alien animal with flailing hooves. The dog avoided the horse's attack and came at Elric's unguarded left side. The albino swung in the saddle and brought his sword hurtling down to slice into the dog's skull and spill brains and blood on the wetly gleaming ground. Still somehow alive, the dog snapped feebly at Elric, but the Melnibonéan ignored its futile attack and turned his attention to the little man who had dispensed with one of his adversaries, but was having difficulty with the second. The dog had grasped the sabre with its beak, gripping the sword near the hilt.

Talons raked towards the little man's throat as he strove to shake the dog's grip. Elric charged forward, his runesword aimed like a lance to where the devil-dog dangled in mid-air, its talons slashing, trying to reach the flesh of its former quarry. Stormbringer caught the beast in its lower abdomen and ripped upwards, slitting the thing's underparts from crutch to throat. It released its hold on the small man's sabre and fell writhing to the ground. Elric's horse trampled it into the rocky ground. Breathing heavily, the albino sheathed Stormbringer and warily regarded the man he had saved. He disliked unnecessary contact with anyone and did not wish to be embarrassed by a display of emotion on the little man's part.

He was not disappointed, for the wide, ugly

mouth split into a cheerful grin and the man bowed in the saddle as he returned his own curved blade to its scabbard.

'Thanks, good sir,' he said lightly. 'Without your help, the battle might have lasted longer. You deprived me of good sport, but you meant well. Moonglum is my name.'

'Elric of Melniboné, I,' replied the albino, but saw no reaction on the little man's face. This was strange, for the name of Elric was now infamous throughout most of the world. The story of his treachery and the slaying of his cousin Cymoril had been told and elaborated upon in taverns throughout the Young Kingdoms. Much as he hated it, he was used to receiving some indication of recognition from those he met. His albinoism was enough to mark him.

Intrigued by Moonglum's ignorance, and feeling strangely drawn towards the cocky little rider, Elric studied him in an effort to discover from what land he came. Moonglum wore no armour and his clothes were of faded blue material, travel-stained and worn. A stout leather belt carried the sabre, a dirk and a woollen purse. Upon his feet, Moonglum wore ankle-length boots of cracked leather. His horse-furniture was much used but of obviously good quality. The man himself, seated high in the saddle, was barely more than five feet tall, with legs too long, in proportion, to the rest of his slight body. His nose was short and uptilted, beneath grey-green eyes, large and innocent-seeming. A mop of vivid red hair fell over his forehead and down his neck, unrestrained. He sat his horse comfortably, still grinning but looking now behind Elric to where Shaarilla rode to join them.

Moonglum bowed elaborately as the girl pulled her horse to a halt.

Elric said coldly, 'The Lady Shaarilla—Master Moonglum of—?'

'Of Elwher,' Moonglum supplied, 'The mercantile capital of the East—the finest city in the world.'

Elric recognised the name. 'So you are from Elwher, Master Moonglum. I have heard of the place. A new city, is it not? Some few centuries old. You have ridden far.'

'Indeed I have, sir. Without knowledge of the language used in these parts, the journey would have been harder, but luckily the slave who inspired me with tales of his homeland taught me the speech thoroughly.'

'But why do you travel these parts—have you not heard the legends?' Shaarilla spoke incredulously.

'Those very legends were what brought me hence—and I'd begun to discount them, until those unpleasant pups set upon me. For what reason they decided to give chase, I will not know, for I gave them no cause to take a dislike to me. This is, indeed, a barbarous land.'

Elric was uncomfortable. Light talk of the kind which Moonglum seemed to enjoy was contrary to his own brooding nature. But in spite of this, he found that he was liking the man more and more.

It was Moonglum who suggested that they travel together for a while. Shaarilla objected, giving Elric a warning glance, but he ignored it.

'Very well then, friend Moonglum, since three are stronger than two, we'd appreciate your company. We ride towards the mountains.' Elric, himself, was feeling in a more cheerful mood.

'And what do you seek there?' Moonglum inquired.

'A secret,' Elric said, and his new-found companion was discreet enough to drop the question.

THREE

~~~~~~~~~~~~~~~~~

So they rode, while the rainfall increased and splashed and sang among the rocks with the sky like dull steel above them and the wind crooning a dirge about their ears. Three small figures riding swiftly towards the black mountain barrier which rose over the world like a brooding God. And perhaps it was a God that laughed sometimes as they neared the foothills of the range, or perhaps it was the wind whistling through the dark mystery of canyons and precipices and the tumble of basalt and granite which climbed towards lonely peaks. Thunder clouds formed around those peaks and lightning smashed downwards like a monster finger searching the earth for grubs. Thunder rattled over the range and Shaarilla spoke her thoughts at last to Elric; spoke them as the mountains came in sight.

'Elric—let us go back, I beg you. Forget the Book—there are too many forces working against us. Take heed of the signs, Elric, or we are doomed!'

But Elric was grimly silent, for he had long been aware that the girl was losing her enthusiasm for the quest she had started.

'Elric—please. We will never reach the Book. Elric, turn back.'

She rode beside him, pulling at his garments until impatiently he shrugged himself clear of her grasp and said:

"I am intrigued too much to stop now. Either continue to lead the way—or tell me what you know and stay here. You desired to sample the Book's wisdom once—but now a few minor pitfalls on our journey have frightened you. What was it you needed to learn, Shaarilla?'

She did not answer him, but said instead: 'And what was it you desired, Elric? Peace, you told me. Well, I warn you, you'll find no peace in those grim mountains—if we reach them at all.'

'You have not been frank with me, Shaarilla,' Elric said coldly, still looking ahead of him at the black peaks. 'You know something of the forces seeking to stop us.'

She shrugged. 'It matters not—I know little. My father spoke a few vague warnings before he died, that is all.'

'What did he say?'

'He said that He who guards the Book would use all his power to stop mankind from using its wisdom.'

'What else?'

'Nothing else. But it is enough, now that I see that my father's warning was truly spoken. It was this guardian who killed him, Elric—or one of the guardian's minions. I do not wish to suffer that fate, in spite of what the Book might do for me. I had thought you powerful enough to aid me—but now I doubt it.'

'I have protected you so far,' Elric said simply. 'Now tell me what you seek from the Book?'

'I am too ashamed.'

Elric did not press the question, but eventually she spoke softly, almost whispering. 'I sought my wings,' she said.

'Your wings—you mean the Book might give you a spell so that you could grow wings!' Elric smiled ironically. 'And that is why you seek the vessel of the world's mightiest wisdom!'

'If you were thought deformed in your own land—it would seem important enough to you,' she shouted defiantly.

Elric turned his face towards her, his crimson-irised eyes burning with a strange emotion. He put a hand to his dead white skin and a crooked smile twisted his lips. 'I, too, have felt as you do,' he said quietly. That was all he said and Shaarilla dropped behind him again, shamed.

They rode on in silence until Moonglum, who had been riding discreetly ahead, cocked his overlarge skull on one side and suddenly drew rein.

Elric joined him. 'What is it, Moonglum?'

'I hear horses coming this way,' the little man said. 'And voices which are disturbingly familiar. More of those devil-dogs, Elric—and this time accompanied by riders!'

Elric, too, heard the sounds, now, and shouted a warning to Shaarilla.

'Perhaps you were right,' he called. 'More trouble comes towards us.'

'What now?' Moonglum said, frowning.

'Ride for the mountains,' Elric replied, 'and we may yet outdistance them.'

They spurred their steeds into a fast gallop and sped towards the hills.

But their flight was hopeless. Soon a black pack was visible on the horizon and the sharp birdlike baying of the devil-dogs drew nearer. Elric stared backward at their pursuers. Night was beginning to fall, and visibility was decreasing with every passing moment but he had a vague impression of the riders who raced behind the pack. They were swathed in dark cloaks and carried long spears. Their faces were invisible, lost in the shadow of the hoods which covered their heads.

Now Elric and his companions were forcing their horses up a steep incline, seeking the shelter of the rocks which lay above.

'We'll halt here,' Elric ordered, 'and try to hold them off. In the open they could easily surround us.'

Moonglum nodded affirmatively, agreeing with the good sense contained in Elric's words. They pulled their sweating steeds to a standstill and prepared to join battle with the howling pack and their dark-cloaked masters.

Soon the first of the devil-dogs were rushing up the incline, their beak-jaws slavering and their talons rattling on stone. Standing between two rocks, blocking the way between with their bodies, Elric and Moonglum met the first attack and quickly dispatched three of the animals. Several more took the place of the dead and the first of the riders was visible behind them as night crept closer.

'Arioch!' swore Elric, suddenly recognising the riders. 'These are the Lords of Dharzi—dead these ten centuries. We're fighting dead men, Moonglum, and the too-tangible ghosts of their dogs. Unless I can think of a sorcerous means to defeat them, we're doomed!'

The zombie-men appeared to have no intention of taking part in the attack for the moment. They waited, their dead eyes eerily luminous, as the devil-dogs attempted to break through the swinging network of steel with which Elric and his companion defended themselves. Elric was racking his brains—trying to dredge a spoken spell from his memory which would dismiss these living dead. Then it came to him, and hoping that the forces he had to invoke would decide to aid him, he began to chant:

'Let the Laws which govern all things
Not so lightly be dismissed;
Let the Ones who flaunt the Earth Kings
With a fresher death be kissed.'

Nothing happened. 'I've failed.' Elric muttered
hopelessly as he met the attack of a snapping devil-
dog and spitted the thing on his sword.

But then—the ground rocked and seemed to *seethe*
beneath the feet of the horses upon whose backs the
dead men sat. The tremor lasted a few seconds and
then subsided.

'The spell was not powerful enough,' Elric sighed.

The earth trembled again and small craters
formed in the ground of the hillside upon which the
dead Lords of Dharzi impassively waited. Stones
crumbled and the horses stamped nervously. Then
the earth rumbled.

'Back!' yelled Elric warningly. 'Back—or we'll go
with them!' They retreated—backing towards Shaarilla and their waiting horses as the ground sagged
beneath their feet. The Dharzi mounts were rearing
and snorting and the remaining dogs turned nervously to regard their masters with puzzled, uncertain eyes. A low moan was coming from the lips of
the living dead. Suddenly, a whole area of the surrounding hillside split into cracks, and yawning
crannies appeared in the surface. Elric and his com-
panies swung themselves on to their horses as, with a
frightful multi-voiced scream, the dead Lords were
swallowed by the earth, returning to the depths from
which they had been summoned.

A deep unholy chuckle arose from the shattered
pit. It was the mocking laughter of the Earth Kings
taking their rightful prey back into their keeping.
Whining, the devil-dogs slunk towards the edge of
the pit, sniffing around it. Then, with one accord,

the black pack hurled itself down into the chasm, following its masters to whatever cold doom awaited them.

Moonglum shuddered. 'You are on familiar terms with the strangest people, friend Elric,' he said shakily and turned his horse towards the mountains again.

They reached the black mountains on the following day and nervously Shaarilla led them along the rocky route she had memorised. She no longer pleaded with Elric to return—she was resigned to whatever fate awaited them. Elric's obsession was burning within him and he was filled with impatience—certain that he would find, at last, the ultimate truth of existence in the Dead Gods' Book. Moonglum was cheerfully sceptical, while Shaarilla was consumed with foreboding.

Rain still fell and the storm growled and crackled above them. And, as the driving rainfall increased with fresh insistence, they came, at last, to the black, gaping mouth of a huge cave.

'I can lead you no further,' Shaarilla said wearily. 'The Book lies somewhere beyond the entrance to this cave.'

Elric and Moonglum looked uncertainly at one another, neither of them sure what move to make next. To have reached their goal seemed somehow anticlimactic—for nothing blocked the cave entrance—and nothing appeared to guard it.

'It is inconceivable,' said Elric, 'that the dangers which beset us were not engineered by something, yet here we are—and no one seeks to stop us entering. Are you sure that this is the *right* cave, Shaarilla?'

The girl pointed upwards to the rock above the entrance. Engraved in it was a curious symbol which Elric instantly recognised.

'The sign of Chaos!' Elric exclaimed. 'Perhaps I should have guessed.'

'What does it mean, Elric?' Moonglum asked.

'That is the symbol of everlasting disruption and anarchy,' Elric told him. 'We are standing in territory presided over by the Lords of Entropy or one of their minions. So that is who our enemy is! This can only mean one thing—the Book is of extreme importance to the order of things on this plane—possibly all the myriad planes of the universe. It was why Arioch was reluctant to aid me—he, too, is a Lord of Chaos!"

Moonglum stared at him in puzzlement. 'What do you mean, Elric?'

'Know you not that two forces govern the world—fighting an eternal battle?' Elric replied. 'Law and Chaos. The upholders of Chaos state that in such a world as they rule, all things are possible. Opponents of Chaos—those who ally themselves with the forces of Law—say that without Law *nothing* material is possible.

"Some stand apart, believing that a balance between the two is the proper state of things, but we cannot. We have become embroiled in a dispute between the two forces. The Book is valuable to either faction, obviously, and I could guess that the minions of Entropy are worried what power we might release if we obtain this Book. Law and Chaos rarely interfere directly in Men's lives—that is why we have not been fully aware of their presence. Now perhaps, I will discover at last the answer to the one question which concerns me—does an ultimate force rule over the opposing factions of Law and Chaos?'

Elric stepped through the cave entrance, peering into the gloom while the others hesitantly followed him.

'The cave stretches back a long way. All we can do is press on until we find its far wall,' Elric said.

'Let's hope that its far wall lies not *downwards*,' Moonglum said ironically as he motioned Elric to lead on.

They stumbled forward as the cave grew darker and darker. Their voices were magnified and hollow to their own ears as the floor of the cave slanted sharply down.

'This is no cave,' Elric whispered, 'it's a *tunnel*— but I cannot guess where it leads.'

For several hours they pressed onwards in pitch darkness, clinging to one another as they reeled forward, uncertain of their footing and still aware that they were moving down a gradual incline. They lost all sense of time and Elric began to feel as if he were living through a dream. Events seemed to have become so unpredictable and beyond his control that he could no longer cope with thinking about them in ordinary terms. The tunnel was long and dark and wide and cold. It offered no comfort and the floor eventually became the only thing which had any reality. It was firmly beneath his feet. He began to feel that possibly he was not moving—that the floor, after all, was moving and he was remaining stationary. His companions clung to him but he was not aware of them. He was lost and his brain was numb. Sometimes he swayed and felt that he was on the edge of a precipice. Sometimes he fell and his groaning body met hard stone, disproving the proximity of the gulf down which he half-expected to fall.

All the while he made his legs perform walking motions, even though he was not at all sure whether he was actually moving forward. And time meant nothing—became a meaningless concept with relation to nothing.

Until, at last, he was aware of a faint, blue glow
ahead of him and he knew that he had been moving
forward. He began to run down the incline, but
found that he was going too fast and had to check his
speed. There was a scent of alien strangeness in the
cool air of the cave tunnel and fear was a fluid force
which surged over him, something separate from
himself.

The others obviously felt it, too, for though they
said nothing, Elric could sense it. Slowly they moved
downward, drawn like automatons towards the pale
blue glow below them.

And then they were out of the tunnel, staring
awestruck at the unearthly vision which confronted
them. Above them, the very air seemed of the
strange blue colour which had originally attracted
them. They were standing on a jutting slab of rock
and, although it was still somehow *dark*, the eerie
blue glow illuminated a stretch of glinting silver
beach beneath them. And the beach was lapped by a
surging dark sea which moved restlessly like a liquid
giant in disturbed slumber. Scattered along the silver beach were the dim shapes of wrecks—the bones
of peculiarly designed boats, each of a different pat-
tern from the rest. The sea surged away into
darkness and there was no horizon—only blackness.
Behind them, they could see a sheer cliff which was
also lost in darkness beyond a certain point. And it
was cold—bitterly cold, with an unbelievable sharp-
ness. For though the sea threshed beneath them, there
was no dampness in the air—no smell of salt. It was a
bleak and awesome sight and, apart from the sea,
they were the only things that moved—the only
things to make sound, for the sea was horribly silent
in its restless movement.

'What now, Elric?' whispered Moonglum, shivering.

Elric shook his head and they continued to stand there for a long time until the albino—his white face and hands ghastly in the alien light said: 'Since it is impracticable to return—we shall venture over the sea.'

His voice was hollow and he spoke as one who was unaware of his words.

Steps, cut into the living rock, led down towards the beach and now Elric began to descend them. The others allowed him to lead them staring around them, their eyes lit by a terrible fascination.

FOUR

~~~~~~~~~~~~~~~

Their feet profaned the silence as they reached
the silver beach of crystalline stones and crunched
across it. Elric's crimson eyes fixed upon one of the
objects littering the beach and he smiled. He shook
his head savagely from side to side, as if to clear it.
Trembling, he pointed to one of the boats, and the
pair saw that it was intact, unlike the others. It was
yellow and red—vulgarly gay in this environment
and nearing it they observed that it was made of
wood, yet unlike any wood they had seen. Moonglum ran his stubby fingers along its length.

'Hard as iron,' he breathed. 'No wonder it has not
rotted as the others have.' He peered inside and
shuddered. 'Well the owner won't argue if we take
it,' he said wryly.

Elric and Shaarilla understood him when they saw
the unnaturally twisted skeleton which lay at the
bottom of the boat. Elric reached inside and pulled
the thing out, hurling it on to the stones. It rattled
and rolled over the gleaming shingle, disintegrating
as it did so, scattering bones over a wide area. The
skull came to rest by the edge of the beach, seeming
to stare sightlessly out over the disturbing ocean.

As Elric and Moonglum strove to push and pull
the boat down the beach towards the sea, Shaarilla
moved ahead of them and squatted down, putting

her hand into the wetness. She stood up sharply, shaking the stuff from her hand.

'This is not water as I know it,' she said. They heard her, but said nothing.

'We'll need a sail,' Elric murmured. The cold breeze was moving out over the ocean. 'A cloak should serve.' He stripped off his cloak and knotted it to the mast of the vessel. 'Two of us will have to hold this at either edge,' he said. 'That way we'll have some slight control over the direction the boat takes. It's makeshift—but the best we can manage.'

They shoved off, taking care not to get their feet in the sea.

The wind caught the sail and pushed the boat out over the ocean, moving at a faster pace than Elric had at first reckoned. The boat began to hurtle forward as if possessed of its own volition and Elric's and Moonglum's muscles ached as they clung to the bottom ends of the sail.

Soon the silver beach was out of sight and they could see little—the pale blue light above them scarcely penetrating the blackness. It was then that they heard the dry flap of wings over their heads and looked up.

Silently descending were three massive ape-like creatures, borne on great leathery wings. Shaarilla recognised them and gasped.

'*Clakars!*'

Moonglum shrugged as he hurriedly drew his sword—'A name only—what are they?' But he received no answer for the leading winged ape descended with a rush, mouthing and gibbering, showing long fangs in a slavering snout. Moonglum dropped his portion of the sail and slashed at the beast but it veered away, its huge wings beating, and sailed upwards again.

Elric unsheathed Stormbringer—and was astound-

ed. The blade remained silent, its familiar howl of
glee muted. The blade shuddered in his hand and
instead of the rush of power which usually flowed up
his arm, he felt only a slight tingling. He was panic-
stricken for a moment—without the sword, he would
soon lose all vitality. Grimly fighting down his fear,
he used the sword to protect himself from the rushing attack of one of the winged apes.

The ape gripped the blade, bowling Elric over,
but it yelled in pain as the blade cut through one
knotted hand, severing fingers which lay twitching
and bloody on the narrow deck. Elric gripped the
side of the boat and hauled himself upright once
more. Shrilling its agony, the winged ape attacked
again, but this time with more caution. Elric summoned all his strength and swung the heavy sword
in a two-handed grip, ripping off one of the leathery
wings so that the mutilated beast flopped about the
deck. Judging the place where its heart should be,
Elric drove the blade in under the breast-bone. The
ape's movements subsided.

Moonglum was lashing wildly at two of the
winged apes which were attacking him from both
sides. He was down on one knee, vainly hacking at
random. He had opened up the whole side of a
beast's head but, though in pain, it still came at him.
Elric hurled Stormbringer through the darkness and
it struck the wounded beast in the throat, point first.
The ape clutched with clawing fingers at the steel
and fell overboard. Its corpse floated on the liquid
but slowly began to sink. Elric grabbed with frantic
fingers at the hilt of his sword, reaching far over the
side of the boat. Incredibly, the blade was sinking
with the beast. Knowing Stormbringer's properties as
he did, Elric was amazed—once when he had hurled
the runesword into the ocean, it had refused to sink.
Now it was being dragged beneath the surface as any

ordinary blade would be dragged. He gripped the hilt and hauled the sword out of the winged ape's carcass.

His strength was seeping swiftly from him. It was incredible. What alien laws governed this cavern world? He could not guess—and all he was concerned with was regaining his waning strength. Without the runesword's power, this was impossible!

Moonglum's curved blade had disembowelled the remaining beast and the little man was busily tossing the dead thing over the side. He turned, grinning triumphantly, to Elric.

'A good fight,' he said.

Elric shook his head. 'We must cross this sea speedily,' he replied, 'else we're lost—finished. My power is gone.'

'How? Why?'

'I know not—unless the forces of Entropy rule more strongly here. Make haste—there is no time for speculation.'

Moonglum's eyes were disturbed. He could do nothing but act as Elric said.

Elric was trembling in his weakness, holding the billowing sail with draining strength. Shaarilla moved to help him, her thin hands close to his; her deep-set eyes bright with sympathy.

'What *were* those things?' Moonglum gasped, his teeth naked and white beneath his back-drawn lips, his breath coming short.

'Clakars,' Shaarilla replied. 'They are the primeval ancestors of my people, older in origin than recorded time. My people are thought the oldest inhabitants of this planet.'

'Whoever seeks to stop us in this quest of yours had best find some—original means.' Moonglum grinned. 'The old methods don't work.' But the other two did not smile, for Elric was half-fainting and the woman was concerned only with his plight. Moonglum shrugged, staring ahead.

When he spoke again, sometime later, his voice was excited. 'We're nearing land!'

Land it was, and they were traveling fast towards it. Too fast. Elric heaved himself upright and spoke heavily and with difficulty. 'Drop the sail!' Moonglum obeyed him. The boat sped on, struck another stretch of silver beach and ground up it, the prow ploughing a dark scar through the glinting shingle. It stopped suddenly, tilting violently to one side so that the three were tumbled against the boat's rail.

Shaarilla and Moonglum pulled themselves upright and dragged the limp and nerveless albino on to the beach. Carrying him between them, they struggled up the beach until the crystalline shingle gave way to thick, fluffy moss, padding their footfalls. They laid the albino down and stared at him worriedly, uncertain of their next actions.

Elric strained to rise, but was unable to do so. 'Give me time,' he gasped. 'I won't die—but already my eyesight is fading. I can only hope that the blade's power will return on dry land.'

With a mighty effort, he pulled Stormbringer from its scabbard and he smiled in relief as the evil runesword moaned faintly and then, slowly, its song increased in power as black flame flickered along its length. Already the power was flowing into Elric's body, giving him renewed vitality. But even as strength returned, Elric's crimson eyes flared with terrible misery.

'Without this black blade,' he groaned, 'I am nothing, as you see. But what is it making of me? Am I to be bound to it for ever?'

The others did not answer him and they were both moved by an emotion they could not define—an

emotion blended of fear, hate and pity—linked with
something else . . .

Eventually, Elric rose, trembling, and silently led
them up the mossy hillside towards a more natural
light which filtered from above. They could see that
it came from a wide chimney, leading apparently to
the upper air. By means of the light, they could soon
make out a dark, irregular shape which towered in
the shadow of the gap.

As they neared the shape, they saw that it was a
castle of black stone—a sprawling pile covered with
dark green crawling lichen which curled over its ancient bulk with an almost sentient protectiveness.
Towers appeared to spring at random from it and it
covered a vast area. There seemed to be no windows
in any part of it and the only orifice was a rearing
doorway blocked by thick bars of a metal which
glowed with dull redness, but without heat. Above
this gate, in flaring amber, was the sign of the Lords
of Entropy, representing eight arrows radiating from
a central hub in all directions. It appeared to hang
in the air without touching the black, lichen-covered
stone.

'I think our quest ends here,' Elric said grimly.
'Here, or nowhere.'

'Before I go further, Elric, I'd like to know what it
is you seek,' Moonglum murmured. 'I think I've
earned the right.'

'A book,' Elric said carelessly. 'The Dead Gods'
Book. It lies within those castle walls—of that I'm
certain. We have reached the end of our journey.'

Moonglum shrugged. 'I might not have asked,' he
smiled, 'for all your words mean to me. I hope that I
will be allowed some small share of whatever
treasure it represents.'

Elric grinned, in spite of the coldness which

gripped his bowels, but he did not answer Moonglum.

'We need to enter the castle, first,' he said instead.

As if the gates had heard him, the metal bars flared to a pale green and then their glow faded back to red and finally dulled into non-existence. The entrance was unbarred and their way apparently clear.

'I like not *that*,' growled Moonglum. 'Too easy. A trap awaits us—are we to spring it at the pleasure of whoever dwells within the castle confines?'

'What else can we do?' Elric spoke quietly.

'Go back—or forward. Avoid the castle—do not tempt He who guards the Book!' Shaarilla was gripping the albino's right arm, her whole face moving with fear, her eyes pleading. 'Forget the Book, Elric!'

'*Now?*' Elric laughed humourlessly. 'Now—after this journey? No, Shaarilla, not when the truth is so close. Better to die than never to have tried to secure the wisdom in the Book when it lies so near.'

Shaarilla's clutching fingers relaxed their grip and her shoulders slumped in hopelessness. 'We cannot do battle with the minions of Entropy . . .'

'Perhaps we will not have to.' Elric did not believe his own words but his mouth was twisted with some dark emotion, intense and terrible. Moonglum glanced at Shaarilla.

'Shaarilla is right,' he said with conviction. 'You'll find nothing but bitterness, possibly death, inside those castle walls. Let us, instead, climb yonder steps and attempt to reach the surface.' He pointed to some twisting steps which led towards the yawning rent in the cavern roof.

Elric shook his head. 'No. You go if you like.'

Moonglum grimaced in perplexity. 'You're a stubborn one, friend Elric. Well, if it's all or nothing—then I'm with you. But personally, I have always preferred compromise.'

Elric began to walk slowly forward towards the dark entrance of the bleak and towering castle.

In a wide, shadowy courtyard a tall figure, wreathed in scarlet fire, stood awaiting them.

Elric marched on, passing the gateway. Moonglum and Shaarilla nervously followed.

Gusty laughter roared from the mouth of the giant and the scarlet fire fluttered about him. He was naked and unarmed, but the power which flowed from him almost forced the three back. His skin was scaly and of smoky purple colouring. His massive body was alive with rippling muscle as he rested lightly on the balls of his feet. His skull was long, slanting sharply backwards at the forehead and his eyes were like slivers of blue steel, showing no pupil. His whole body shook with mighty, malicious joy.

'Greetings to you, Lord Elric of Melniboné—I congratulate you for your remarkable tenacity!'

'Who are you?' Elric growled, his hand on his sword.

'My name is Orunlu the Keeper and this is a stronghold of the Lords of Entropy.' The giant smiled cynically. 'You need not finger your puny blade so nervously, for you should know that I cannot harm you now. I gained power to remain in your realm only by making that vow.'

Elric's voice betrayed his mounting excitement. 'You cannot stop us?'

'I do not dare to—since my oblique efforts have failed. But your foolish endeavours perplex me somewhat, I'll admit. The Book is of importance to us—but what can it mean to you? I have guarded it for three hundred centuries and have never been curious enough to seek to discover why my Masters place so much importance upon it—why they bothered to rescue it on its sunward course and incarcerate it on this boring ball of earth populated by the capering, briefly-lived clowns called Men?'

'I seek in it the Truth,' Elric said guardedly.

'*There is no Truth but that of Eternal struggle,*' the scarlet-flamed giant said with conviction.

'What rules above the forces of Law and Chaos?' Elric asked. 'What controls your destinies as it controls mine?'

The giant frowned.

'*That question, I cannot answer. I do not know. There is only the Balance.*'

'Then perhaps the Book will tell us who holds it.' Elric said purposefully. 'Let me pass—tell me where it lies.'

The giant moved back, smiling ironically. '*It lies in a small chamber in the central tower. I have sworn never to venture there, otherwise I might even lead the way. Go if you like—my duty is over.*'

Elric, Moonglum and Shaarilla stepped towards the entrance of the castle, but before they entered, the giant spoke warningly from behind them.

'*I have been told that the knowledge contained in the Book could swing the balance on the side of the forces of Law. This disturbs me—but, it appears, there is another possibility which disturbs me even more.*'

'What is that?' Elric said.

'*It could create such a tremendous impact on the multiverse that complete entropy would result. My Masters do not desire that—for it could mean the destruction of all matter in the end. We exist only to fight—not to win, but to preserve the eternal struggle.*'

'I care not,' Elric told him. 'I have little to lose, Orunlu the Keeper.'

'*Then go.*' The giant strode across the courtyard into blackness.

Inside the tower, light of a pale quality illuminated winding steps leading upwards. Elric began to climb them in silence, moved by his own doom-filled purpose. Hesitantly, Moonglum and Shaarilla followed in his path, their faces set in hopeless acceptance.

On and upward the steps mounted, twisting tortuously towards their goal, until at last they came to the chamber, full of blinding light, many-coloured and scintillating, which did not penetrate outwards at all but remained confined to the room which housed it.

Blinking, shielding his red eyes with his arm, Elric pressed forward and, through slitted pupils saw the source of the light lying on a small stone dais in the centre of the room.

Equally troubled by the bright light, Shaarilla and Moonglum followed him into the room and stood in awe at what they saw.

It was a huge book—the Dead Gods' Book, its covers encrusted with alien gems from which the light sprang. It gleamed, it *throbbed* with light and brilliant colour.

'At last,' Elric breathed, 'At last—the Truth!'

He stumbled forward like a man made stupid with drink, his pale hands reaching for the thing he had sought with such savage bitterness. His hands touched the pulsating cover of the Book and, trembling, turned it back.

'Now, I shall learn,' he said, half-gloatingly.

With a crash, the cover fell to the floor, sending the bright gems skipping and dancing over the paving stones.

Beneath Elric's twitching hands lay nothing but a pile of yellowish dust.

'No!' His scream was anguished, unbelieving. 'No!' Tears flowed down his contorted face as he ran his hands through the fine dust. With a groan which racked his whole being, he fell forward, his face hitting the disintegrated parchment. Time had destroyed the Book—untouched, possibly forgotten, for three hundred centuries. Even the wise and powerful Gods who had created it had perished—and now its knowledge followed them into oblivion.

They stood on the slopes of the high mountain, staring down into the green valleys below them. The sun shone and the sky was clear and blue. Behind them lay the gaping hole which led into the stronghold of the Lords of Entropy.

Elric looked with sad eyes across the world and his head was lowered beneath a weight of weariness and dark despair. He had not spoken since his companions had dragged him sobbing from the chamber of the Book. Now he raised his pale face and spoke in a voice tinged with self-mockery, sharp with bitterness—a lonely voice: the calling of hungry seabirds circling cold skies above bleak shores.

'Now,' he said, 'I will live my life without ever knowing why I live it—whether it has purpose or not. Perhaps the Book could have told me. But would I have believed it, even then? I am the eternal sceptic—never *sure* that my actions are my own; never certain that an ultimate entity is not guiding me.

'I envy those who know. All I can do now is to continue my quest and hope, without hope, that before my span is ended, the truth will be presented to me.'

Shaarilla took his limp hands in hers and her eyes were wet.

'Elric—let me comfort you.'

The albino sneered bitterly. 'Would that we'd never met, Shaarilla of the Dancing Mist. For a while, you gave me hope—I had thought to be at last at peace with myself. But, because of you, I am left

more hopeless than before. There is no salvation in
this world—only malevolent doom. Goodbye.'

He took his hands away from her grasp and set off
down the mountainside.

Moonglum darted a glance at Shaarilla and then
at Elric. He took something from his purse and put
it in the girl's hand.

'Good luck,' he said, and then he was running after Elric until he caught him up.

Still striding, Elric turned at Moonglum's ap-
proach and, despite his brooding misery said: 'What
is it, friend Moonglum? Why do you follow me?'

'I've followed you thus far, Master Elric, and I see
no reason to stop,' grinned the little man. 'Besides,
unlike yourself, I'm a materialist. We'll need to eat,
you know.'

Elric frowned, feeling a warmth growing within
him. 'What do you mean, Moonglum?'

Moonglum chuckled. 'I take advantage of situa-
tions of any kind, where I may,' he answered. He
reached into his purse and displayed something on
his outstretched hand which shone with a dazzling
brilliancy. It was one of the jewels from the cover of
the Book. 'There are more in my purse,' he said,
'And each one worth a fortune.' He took Elric's arm.

'Come, Elric—what new lands shall we visit so that
we may change these baubles into wine and pleasant
company?'

Behind them, standing stock still on the hillside,
Shaarilla stared miserably after them until they were
no longer visible. The jewel Moonglum had given
her dropped from her fingers and fell, bouncing and
bright, until it was lost amongst the heather. Then
she turned—and the dark mouth of the cavern yawned
before her.

Book Three

THE SINGING CITADEL

In which Elric has his first dealings with Pan Tang, Yishana of Jharkor, the sorcerer Theleb K'aarna, and learns something more of the Higher Worlds . . .

ONE

The turquoise sea was peaceful in the golden light of early evening, and the two men at the rail of the ship stood in silence, looking north to the misty horizon. One was tall and slim, wrapped in a heavy black cloak, its cowl flung back to reveal his long, milk-white hair; the other was short and red-headed.

'She was a fine woman and she loved you,' said the short man at length. 'Why did you leave her so abruptly?'

'She was a fine woman,' the tall one replied, 'but she would have loved me to her cost. Let her seek her own land and stay there. I have already slain one woman whom I loved, Moonglum. I would not slay another.'

Moonglum shrugged. 'I sometimes wonder, Elric, if this grim destiny of yours is the figment of your own guilt-ridden mood.'

'Perhaps,' Elric replied carelessly. 'But I do not care to test the theory. Let's speak no more of this.'

The sea foamed and rushed by as the oars disrupted the surface, driving the ship swiftly towards the port of Dhakos, capital of Jharkor, one of the most powerful of the Young Kingdoms. Less than two years previously Jharkor's king, Darmit, had died in the ill-fated raid on Imrryr, and Elric had heard that the men of Jharkor blamed him for the young king's death, though this was not the case. He cared little whether they blamed him or not, for he was still disdainful of the greater part of mankind.

'Another hour will see nightfall, and it's unlikely we'll sail at night,' Moonglum said. 'I'll to bed, I think.'

Elric was about to reply when he was interrupted by a high-pitched shout from the crowsnest.

'Sail on larboard stern!'

The lookout must have been half asleep, for the ship bearing down on them could easily be made out from the deck. Elric stepped aside as the captain, a dark-faced Tarkeshite, came running along the deck.

'What's the ship, captain?' called Moonglum.

'A Pan Tang trireme—a warship. They're on ramming course.' The captain ran on, yelling orders to the helm to turn the ship aside.

Elric and Moonglum crossed the deck to see the trireme better. She was a black-sailed ship, painted black and heavily gilded, with three rowers to an oar as against their two. She was big and yet elegant, with a high curving stern and a low prow. Now they could see the waters broken by her big, brass-sheathed ram. She had two lateen-rigged sails, and the wind was in her favour.

The rowers were in a panic as they sweated to turn the ship according to the helmsman's orders. Oars rose and fell in confusion and Moonglum turned to Elric with a half-smile.

'They'll never do it. Best ready your blade, friend.'

Pan Tang was an isle of sorcerers, fully human, who sought to emulate the old power of Melniboné. Their fleets were among the best in the Young Kingdoms and raided with little discrimination. The Theocrat of Pan Tang, chief of the priest-aristocracy, was Jagreen Lern, who was reputed to have a pact with the powers of Chaos and a plan to rule the world.

Elric regarded the men of Pan Tang as upstarts who could never hope to mirror the glory of his ancestors, but even he had to admit that this ship was impressive and would easily win a fight with the Tarkeshite galley.

Soon the great trireme was bearing down on them and captain and helmsman fell silent as they realised they could not evade the ram. With a harsh sound of crushed timbers, the ram connected with the stern, holing the galley beneath the waterline.

Elric stood immobile, watching as the trireme's grappling irons hurtled towards their galley's deck. Somewhat half-heartedly, knowing they were no match for the well-trained and well-armoured Pan Tang crew, the Tarkeshites ran towards the stern, preparing to resist the boarders.

Moonglum cried urgently: 'Elric—we must help!'

Reluctantly Elric nodded. He was loathe to draw the runesword from its scabbard at his side. Of late its power seemed to have increased.

Now the scarlet-armoured warriors were swinging towards where the Tarkeshites waited. The first wave, armed with broadswords and battle-axes, hit the sailors, driving them back.

Now Elric's hand fell to the hilt of Stormbringer. As he gripped it and drew it, the blade gave an odd, disturbing moan, as if of anticipation, and a weird black radiance flickered along its length. Now it throbbed in Elric's hand like something alive as the albino ran forward to aid the Tarkeshite sailors.

Already half the defenders had been hewed down and as the rest retreated, Elric, with Moonglum at his heels, moved forward. The scarlet-armoured warriors' expressions changed from grim triumph to startlement as Elric's great black-blade shrieked up and down and clove through a man's armour from shoulder to lower ribs.

Evidently they recognized him and the sword, for both were legendary. Though Moonglum was a skilled swordsman, they all but ignored him as they realised that they must concentrate all their strength on bringing Elric down if they were to survive.

The old, wild killing-lust of his ancestors now dominated Elric as the blade reaped souls. He and the sword became one and it was the sword, not Elric, that was in control. Men fell on all sides, screaming more in horror than in pain as they realised what the sword had drawn from them. Four came at him with axes whistling. He sliced off one's head, cut a deep gash in another's midriff, lopped off an arm, and drove the blade point first into the heart of the last. Now the Tarkeshites were cheering, following after Elric and Moonglum as they cleared the sinking galley's decks of attackers.

Howling like a wolf, Elric grabbed a rope—part of the black and gold trireme's rigging—and swung towards the enemy's decks.

'Follow him!' Moonglum yelled. 'This is our only chance—this ship's doomed!'

The trireme had raised decks fore and aft. On the foredeck stood the captain, splendid in scarlet and blue, his face aghast at this turn of events. He had expected to get his prize effortlessly, now it seemed *he* was to be the prize!

Stormbringer sang a wailing song as Elric pressed towards the foredeck, a song that was at once triumphant and ecstatic. The remaining warriors no longer rushed at him, and concentrated on Moonglum, who was leading the Tarkeshite crew, leaving Elric's path to the captain clear.

The captain, a member of the theocracy, would be harder to vanquish than his men. As Elric moved towards him, he noted that the man's armour had a peculiar glow to it—it had been sorcerously treated.

The captain was typical of his kind—stocky, heavily-bearded, with malicious black eyes over a strong, hooked nose. His lips were thick and red and he was smiling a little as, with axe in one hand and sword in the other, he prepared to meet Elric, who was running up the steps.

Elric gripped Stormbringer in both hands and lunged for the captain's stomach, but the man stepped sideways and parried with his sword, swinging the axe left-handed at Elric's unprotected head. The albino had to sway to one side, staggered, and fell to the deck, rolling as the broadsword thudded into the deck, just missing his shoulder. Stormbringer seemed to rise of its own accord to block a further axe blow and then chopped upwards to sheer off the head near the handle. The captain cursed and discarded the handle, gripped his broadsword in both hands and raised it. Again Stormbringer acted a fraction sooner than Eric's own reactions. He drove the blade up towards the man's heart. The magic-treated armour stopped it for a second; but then Stormbringer shrilled a chilling, wailing song, shuddered as if summoning more strength, slipped on the armour again. And then the magic armour split like a nutshell, leaving Elric's opponent bare-chested, his arms still raised for the strike. His eyes widened. He backed away, his sword forgotten, his gaze fixed on the evil runeblade as it struck him under the breastbone and drove in. He grimaced, whimpered, and dropped his sword, clutching instead at the blade, which was sucking out his soul.

'By Chardros—not—not—aahhh!'

He died knowing that even his soul was not safe from the hell-blade borne by the wolf-faced albino.

Elric wrenched Stormbringer from the corpse, feeling his own vitality increase as the sword passed on its stolen energy, refusing to consider the knowledge that he needed the sword the more he used it.

On the deck of the trireme, only the galley-slaves were left alive. But the deck was tilting badly, for the trireme's ram and grapples still tied it to the sinking Tarkeshite ship.

'Cut the grappling ropes and back water—quickly!' Elric yelled. Sailors, realising what was happening, leapt forward to do as he ordered. The slaves backed water, and the ram came out with a groan of split wood. The grapples were cut and the doomed galley set adrift.

Elric counted the survivors. Less than half the crew were alive, and their captain had died in the first onslaught. He addressed the slaves.

'If you'd have your freedom, row well towards Dhakos,' he called. The sun was setting, but now that he was in command he decided to sail through the night by the stars.

Moonglum shouted incredulously: 'Why offer them their freedom? We could sell them in Dhakos and thus be paid for today's exertion!'

Elric shrugged. 'I offer them freedom because I choose to, Moonglum.'

The redhead sighed and turned to supervise the throwing of the dead and wounded overboard. He would never understand the albino, he decided. It was probably for the best.

And that was how Elric came to enter Dhakos in some style, when he had originally intended to slip into the city without being recognised.

Leaving Moonglum to negotiate the sale of the trireme and divide the money between the crew and himself, Elric drew his hood over his head and pushed through the crowd which had collected, making for an inn he knew of by the west gate of the city.

TWO

~~~~~~~~~~~~~~~~

Later that night, when Moonglum had gone to bed, Elric sat in the tavern room drinking. Even the most enthusiastic of the night's roisterers had left when they had noticed with whom they shared the room; and now Elric sat alone, the only light coming from a guttering reed torch over the outside door.

Now the door opened and a richly-dressed youth stood there, staring in.

'I seek the White Wolf,' he said, his head at a questioning angle. He could not see Elric clearly.

'I'm sometimes called that name in these parts,' Elric said calmly. 'Do you seek Elric of Melniboné?'

'Aye. I have a message.' The youth came in, keeping his cloak wrapped about him, for the room was cold though Elric did not notice it.

'I am Count Yolan, deputy-commander of the city guard,' the youth said arrogantly, coming up to the table at which Elric sat and studying the albino rudely. 'You are brave to come here so openly. Do you think the folk of Jharkor have such short memories they can forget that you led their king into a trap scarce two years since?'

Elric sipped his wine, then said from behind the rim of his cup: 'This is rhetoric, Count Yolan. What is your message?'

Yolan's assured manner left him; he made a rather weak gesture. 'Rhetoric to you, perhaps—but I for

one feel strongly on the matter. Would not King
Darmit be here today if you had not fled from the
battle that broke the power of the Sea Lords and
your own folk? Did you not use your sorcery to aid
you in your flight, instead of using it to aid the men
who thought they were your comrades?'

Elric sighed. 'I know your purpose here was not to
bait me in this manner. Darmit died on board his
flagship during the first attack on Imrryr's sea-maze,
not in the subsequent battle.'

'You sneer at my questions and then proffer lame
lies to cover your own cowardly deed,' Yolan said
bitterly. 'If I had my way you'd be fed to your hell-
blade there—I've heard what happened earlier.'

Elric rose slowly. 'Your taunts tire me. When you
feel ready to deliver your message, give it to the
inn-keeper.'

He walked around the table, moving towards the
stairs, but stopped as Yolan turned and plucked at
his sleeve.

Elric's corpse-white face stared down at the young
noble. His crimson eyes flickered with a dangerous
emotion. 'I am not used to such familiarity, young
man.'

Yolan's hand fell away. 'Forgive me. I was self-in-
dulgent and should not have let my emotions over-
ride diplomacy. I came on a matter of discretion—a
message from Queen Yishana. She seeks your help.'

'I'm as disinclined to help others as I am to explain my actions,' Elric spoke impatiently. 'In the
past my help has not always been to the advantage of
those who've sought it. Darmit, your queen's half-
brother, discovered that.'

Yolan said sullenly: 'You echo my own warnings to
the queen, sir. For all that, she desires to see you in
private—tonight . . .' he scowled and looked away. 'I

would point out that I could have you arrested should you refuse.'

'Perhaps.' Elric moved again towards the steps. 'Tell Yishana that I stay the night here and move on at dawn. She may visit me if her request is so urgent.' He climbed the stairs, leaving a gape-mouthed Yolan sitting alone in the quiet of the tavern.

Theleb K'aarna scowled. For all his skill in the black arts, he was a fool in love; and Yishana, sprawled on her fur-rich bed, knew it. It pleased her to have power over a man who could destroy her with a simple incantation if it were not for his love-weakness. Though Theleb K'aarna stood high in the hierarchy of Pan Tang, it was clear to her that she was in no danger from the sorcerer. Indeed, her intuition informed her that this man who loved to dominate others also needed to be dominated. She filled this need for him—with relish.

Theleb K'aarna continued to scowl at her. 'How can that decadent spell-singer help you where I cannot?' he muttered, sitting down on the bed and stroking her bejewelled foot.

Yishana was not a young woman, neither was she pretty. Yet there was an hypnotic quality about her tall, full body, her lush black hair, and her wholly sensuous face. Few of the men she had singled out for her pleasure had been able to resist her.

Neither was she sweet-natured, just, wise, nor self-sacrificing. The historians would append no noble soubriquet to her name. Still, there was something so self-sufficient about her, something denying the usual standards by which a person was judged, that all who knew her admired her, and she was well-loved by those she ruled—loved rather as a wilful child is loved, yet loved with firm loyalty.

Now she laughed quietly, mockingly at her sorcerer lover.

'You're probably right, Theleb K'aarna, but Elric is a legend—the most spoken-of, least-known man in the world. This is my opportunity to discover what others have only speculated on—his true character.'

Theleb K'aarna made a pettish gesture. He stroked his long black beard and got up, walking to a table bearing fruit and wine. He poured wine for them both. 'If you seek to make me jealous again, you are succeeding, of course. I hold little hope for your ambition. Elric's ancestors were half-demons—his race is not human and cannot be judged by our yardsticks. To us, sorcery is learned after years of study and sacrifice—to Elric's kind, sorcery is intuitive—natural. You may not live to learn his secrets. Cymoril, his beloved cousin, died on his blade—and she was his betrothed!'

'Your concern is touching.' She lazily accepted the goblet he handed to her. 'But I'll continue with my plan, none the less. After all, you can hardly claim to have had much success in discovering the nature of this citadel!'

'There are subtleties I have not properly plumbed as yet!'

'Then perhaps Elric's intuition will provide answers where you fail,' she smiled. Then he got up and looked through the window at the sky where the full moon hung in a clear sky over the spires of Dhakos. 'Yolan is late. If all went properly, he should have brought Elric here by now.'

'Yolan was a mistake. You should not have sent such a close friend of Darmit's. For all we know, he's challenged Elric and killed him!'

Again she couldn't resist laughter. 'Oh, you wish too hard—it clouds your reason. I sent Yolan because I knew he would be rude to the albino and perhaps weaken his usual insouciance—arouse his curiosity. Yolan was a kind of bait to bring Elric to us!'

'Then possibly Elric sensed this?'

'I am not overly intelligent, my love—but I think my instincts rarely betray me. We shall see soon.'

A little later there was a discreet scratch at the door and a handmaiden entered.

'Your Highness, Count Yolan has returned.'

'Only Count Yolan?' There was a smile on Theleb K'aarna's face. It was to disappear in a short while as Yishana left the room, garbed for the street.

'You are a fool!' he snarled as the door slammed. He flung down his goblet. Already he had been unsuccessful in the matter of the citadel and, if Elric displaced him, he could lose everything. He began to think very deeply, very carefully.

THREE

~~~~~~~~~~~~~

Though he claimed lack of conscience, Elric's tormented eyes belied the claim as he sat at his window, drinking strong wine and thinking on the past. Since the sack of Imrryr, he had quested the world, seeking some purpose to his existence, some meaning to his life.

He had failed to find the answer in the Dead God's Book. He had failed to love Shaarilla, the wingless woman of Myyrrhn, failed to forget Cymoril, who still inhabited his nightmares. And there were memories of other dreams—of a fate he dare not think upon.

Peace, he thought, was all he sought. Yet even peace in death was denied him. It was in this mood that he continued to brood until his reverie was broken by a soft scratching at the door.

Immediately his expression hardened. His crimson eyes took on a guarded look, his shoulders lifted so that when he stood up he was all cool arrogance. He placed the cup on the table and said lightly:

'Enter!'

A woman entered, swathed in a dark red cloak, unrecognisable in the gloom of the room. She closed the door behind her and stood there, motionless and unspeaking.

When at length she spoke, her voice was almost hesitant, though there was some irony in it, too.

'You sit in darkness, Lord Elric, I had thought to find you asleep ...'

'Sleep, madam, is the occupation that bores me most. But I will light a torch if you find the darkness unattractive.' He went to the table and removed the cover from the small bowl of charcoal which lay there. He reached for a thin wooden spill and placed one end in the bowl, blowing gently. Soon the charcoal glowed, and the taper caught, and he touched it to a reed torch that hung in a bracket on the wall above the table.

The torch flared and sent shadows skipping around the small chamber. The woman drew back her cowl and the light caught her dark, heavy features and the masses of black hair which framed them. She contrasted strongly with the slender, aesthetic albino who stood a head taller, looking at her impassively.

She was unused to impassive looks and the novelty pleased her.

'You sent for me, Lord Elric—and you see I am here.' She made a mock curtsey.

'Queen Yishana,' he acknowledged the curtsey with a slight bow. Now that she confronted him, she sensed his power—a power that perhaps attracted even more strongly than her own. And yet, he gave no hint that he responded to her. She reflected that a situation she had expected to be interesting might, ironically, become frustrating. Even this amused her.

Elric, in turn, was intrigued by this woman in spite of himself. His jaded emotions hinted that Yishana might restore their edge. This excited him and perturbed him at once.

He relaxed a little and shrugged. 'I have heard of you, Queen Yishana, in other lands than Jharkor. Sit down if you wish.' He indicated a bench and seated himself on the edge of the bed.

'You are more courteous than your summons suggested,' she smiled as she sat down, crossed her legs, and folded her arms in front of her. 'Does this mean that you will listen to a proposition I have?'

He smiled back. It was a rare smile for him, a little grim, but without the usual bitterness. 'I think so. You are an unusual woman, Queen Yishana. Indeed, I would suspect that you had Melnibonéan blood if I did not know better.'

'Not all your Young Kingdom "upstarts" are quite as unsophisticated as you believe, my lord.'

'Perhaps.'

'Now that I see you at last, face to face, I find your dark legend a little hard to credit in parts—and yet, on the other hand,' she put her head on one side and regarded him frankly, 'it would seem that the legends speak of a less subtle man than the one I see before me.'

'That is the way with legends.'

'Ah,' she half-whispered, 'what a force we could be together, you and I . . .'

'Speculation of that sort irritates me, Queen Yishana. What is your purpose in coming here?'

'Very well, I did not expect you to listen, even.'

'I'll listen—but expect nothing more.'

'Then listen. I think the story will be appreciated, even by you.'

Elric listened and, as Yishana had suspected, the tale she told began to catch his interest . . .

Several months ago, Yishana told Elric, peasants in the Gharavian province of Jharkor began to talk of some mysterious riders who were carrying off young men and women from the villages.

Suspecting bandits, Yishana had sent a detachment of her White Leopards, Jharkor's finest fighting men, to the province to put down the brigands.

None of the White Leopards had returned. A second expedition had found no trace of them but, in a valley close to the town of Thokora, they had come upon a strange citadel. Descriptions of the citadel were confused. Suspecting that the White Leopards had attacked and been defeated, the officer in charge had used discretion, left a few men to watch the citadel and report anything they saw, and returned at once to Dhakos. One thing was certain—the citadel had not been in the valley a few months before.

Yishana and Theleb K'aarna had led a large force to the valley. The men left behind had disappeared but, as soon as he saw the citadel, Theleb K'aarna had warned Yishana not to attack.

'It was a marvellous sight, Lord Elric,' Yishana continued. 'The citadel scintillated with shining, rainbow colours—colours that were constantly altering, changing. The whole building looked unreal—sometimes it stood out sharply; sometimes it seemed misty, as if about to vanish. Theleb K'aarna said its nature was sorcerous, and we did not doubt him. Something from the Realm of Chaos, he said, and that seemed likely.' She got up.

She spread her hands. 'We are not used to large-scale manifestations of sorcery in these parts. Theleb K'aarna was familiar enough with sorcery—he comes from the City of Screaming Statues on Pan Tang, and such things are seen frequently—but even he was taken aback.'

'So you withdrew,' Elric prompted impatiently.

'We were about to—in fact Theleb K'aarna and myself were already riding back at the head of the army when the music came ... It was sweet, beautiful, unearthly, painful—Theleb K'aarna shouted to me to ride as swiftly as I could away from it. I dallied, attracted by the music, but he slapped the rump of my horse and we rode, fast as dragons in flight, away from there. Those nearest us also escaped—but we saw the rest turn and move back towards the citadel, drawn by the music. Nearly two hundred men went back—and vanished.'

'What did you do then?' Elric asked as Yishana crossed the floor and sat down beside him. He moved to give her more room.

'Theleb K'aarna has been trying to investigate the nature of the citadel—its purpose and its controller. So far, his divinations have told him little more than he guessed: that the Realm of Chaos has sent the citadel to the Realm of Earth and is slowly extending its range. More and more of our young men and women are being abducted by the minions of Chaos.'

'And these minions?' Yishana had moved a little closer, and this time Elric did not move away.

'None who has sought to stop them has succeeded— few have lived.'

'And what do you seek of me?'

'Help.' She looked closely into his face and reached out a hand to touch him. 'You have knowledge of both Chaos and Law—old knowledge, instinctive knowledge if Theleb K'aarna is right. Why, your very Gods are Lords of Chaos.'

'That is exactly true, Yishana—and because our patron Gods are of Chaos, it is not in my interest to fight against any one of them.'

Now he moved towards her and he was smiling, looking into her eyes. Suddenly, he took her in his arms. 'Perhaps you will be strong enough,' he said enigmatically, just before their lips met. 'And as for the other matter—we can discuss that later.'

In the deep greenness of a dark mirror, Theleb K'aarna saw something of the scene in Elric's room and he glowered impotently. He tugged at his beard as the scene faded for the tenth time in a minute.

None of his mutterings could restore it. He sat back in his chair of serpent skulls and planned vengeance. That vengeance could take time maturing, he decided; for, if Elric could be useful in the matter of the citadel, there was no point in destroying him yet. . . .

FOUR

~~~~~~~~~~~~~~~~~~

Next afternoon, three riders set off for the town of
Thokora. Elric and Yishana rode close together; but
the third rider, Theleb K'aarna, kept a frowning distance. If Elric was at all embarrassed by this display
on the part of the man he had ousted in Yishana's af-
fections, he did not show it.

Elric, finding Yishana more than attractive in spite
of himself, had agreed at least to inspect the citadel
and suggest what it might be and how it might be
fought. He had exchanged a few words with Moonglum before setting off.

They rode across the beautiful grasslands of
Jharkor, golden beneath a hot sun. It was two days'
ride to Thokora, and Elric intended to enjoy it.

Feeling less than miserable, he galloped along
with Yishana, laughing with her in her enjoyment.
Yet, buried deeper than it would normally have
been, there was a deep forboding in his heart as
they neared the mysterious citadel, and he noted
that Theleb K'aarna occasionally looked satisfied
when he should have looked disgruntled.

Sometimes Elric would shout to the sorcerer. 'Ho,
old spell-maker, do you feel no joyful release from
the cares of the court out here amidst the beauties of
nature? Your face is long, Theleb K'aarna—breathe
in the untainted air and laugh with us!' Then The-

leb K'aarna would scowl and mutter, and Yishana
would laugh at him and glance brightly at Elric.

So they came to Thokora and found it a smoulder-
ing pit that stank like a midden of hell.

Elric sniffed. 'This is Chaos work. You were right
enough there, Theleb K'aarna. Whatever fire destroyed such a large town, it was not natural fire.
Whoever is responsible for this is evidently increas-
ing his power. As you know, sorcerer, the Lords of
Law and Chaos are usually in perfect balance, neither tampering directly with our Earth. Evidently
the balance has tipped a little way to one side, as it
sometimes does, favouring the Lords of Disorder—al-
lowing them access to our realm. Normally it is possible for an earthly sorcerer to summon aid from
Chaos or Law for a short time, but it is rare for either
side to establish itself so firmly as our friend in the
citadel evidently has. What is more disturbing—for
you of the Young Kingdoms, at least—is that, once
such power is gained, it is possible to increase it, and
the Lords of Chaos could in time conquer the Realm
of Earth by gradual increase of their strength here.'

'A terrible possibility,' muttered the sorcerer, genuinely afraid. Even though he could sometimes summon help from Chaos, it was in no human being's
interest to have Chaos ruling over him.

Elric climbed back into his saddle. 'We'd best
make speed to the valley,' he said.

'Are you sure it is wise, after witnessing this?'
Theleb K'aarna was nervous.

Elric laughed. 'What? And you a sorcerer from
Pan Tang—that isle that claims to know as much of
sorcery as my ancestors, the Bright Emperors! No,
no—besides, I'm not in a cautious mood today!'

'Nor am I,' cried Yishana, clapping her steed's
sides. 'Come, gentlemen—to the Citadel of Chaos!'

By late afternoon, they had topped the range of hills surrounding the valley and looked down at the mysterious citadel.

Yishana had described it well—but not perfectly. Elric's eyes ached as he looked at it, for it seemed to extend beyond the Realm of Earth into a different plane, perhaps several.

It shimmered and glittered and all Earthly colours were there, as well as many which Elric recognised as belonging to other planes. Even the basic outline of the citadel was uncertain. In contrast, the surrounding valley was a sea of dark ash, which sometimes seemed to eddy, to undulate and send up spurting geysers of dust, as if the basic elements of nature had been disturbed, and warped by the presence of the supernatural citadel.

'Well?' Theleb K'aarna tried to calm his nervous horse as it backed away from the citadel. 'Have you seen the like in the world before?'

Elric shook his head. 'Not in this world, certainly; but I've seen it before. During my final initiation into the arts of Melniboné, my father took me with him in astral form to the Realm of Chaos, there to receive the audience of my patron the Lord Arioch of the Seven Darks . . .'

Theleb K'aarna shuddered. 'You have been to Chaos? It is Arioch's citadel, then?'

Elric laughed in disdain. 'That! No, it is a hovel compared to the palaces of the Lords of Chaos.'

Impatiently, Yishana said; 'Then who dwells *there*?'

'As I remember, the one who dwelt in the citadel when I passed through the Chaos Realm in my youth—he was no Lord of Chaos, but a kind of servant to the Lords. Yet,' he frowned, 'not exactly a servant. . . .'

'*Ach!* You speak in riddles.' Theleb K'aarna

turned his horse to ride down the hills, away from the citadel. 'I know you Melnibonéans! Starving, you'd rather have a paradox than food!'

Elric and Yishana followed him some distance, then Elric stopped. Elric pointed behind him.

'The one who dwells yonder is a paradoxical sort of fellow. He's a kind of Jester to the Court of Chaos. The Lords of Chaos respect him—perhaps fear him slightly—even though he entertains them. He delights them with cosmic riddles, with farcical satires purporting to explain the nature of the Cosmic Hand that holds both Chaos and Law in balance, he juggles enigmas like baubles, laughs at what Chaos holds dear, takes seriously that which they mock at . . .' He paused and shrugged. 'So I have heard, at least.'

'Why should he be here?'

'Why should he be anywhere? I could guess at the motives of Chaos or Law and probably be right. But not even the Lords of the Higher Worlds can understand the motives of Balo the Jester. It is said that he is the only one allowed to move between the Realms of Chaos and Law at will, though I have never heard of him coming to the Realm of Earth before. Neither, for that matter, have I ever heard him credited with such acts of destruction as that which we've witnessed. It is a puzzle to me—one which would no doubt please him if he knew.'

'There would be one way of discovering the purpose of his visit,' Theleb K'aarna said with a faint smile. 'If someone entered the citadel . . .'

'Come now, sorcerer,' Elric mocked. 'I've little love for life, to be sure, but there are some things of value to me—my soul, for one!'

Theleb K'aarna began to ride on down the hill, but Elric remained thoughtfully where he was, Yishana beside him.

'You seem more troubled by this than you should be, Elric,' she said.

'It *is* disturbing. There is a hint here that, if we investigate the citadel further, we should become embroiled in some dispute between Balo and his masters—perhaps even the Lords of Law, too. To become so involved could easily mean our destruction, since the forces at work are more dangerous and powerful than anything we are familiar with on Earth.'

'But we cannot simply watch this Balo laying our cities waste, carrying off our fairest, threatening to rule Jharkor himself within a short time!'

Elric sighed, but did not reply.

'Have you no sorcery, Elric, to send Balo back to Chaos where he belongs, to seal the breach he has made in our Realm?'

'Even Melnibonéans cannot match the power of the Lords of the Higher Worlds—and my forefathers knew much more of sorcery than do I. My best allies serve neither Chaos nor Law, they are elementals: lords of fire, earth, air, and water, entities with affinities with beasts and plants. Good allies in an earthly battle—but of no great use when matched against one such as Balo. I must think. . . . At least, if I opposed Balo it would not necessarily incur the wrath of my patron Lords. Something, I suppose. . . .'

The hills rolled green and lush to the grasslands at their feet, the sun beat down from a clear sky on the infinity of grass stretching to the horizon. Above them a large predatory bird wheeled; and Theleb K'aarna was a tiny figure, turning in the saddle to call to them in a thin voice, but his words could not be heard.

Yishana seemed dispirited. Her shoulders slightly slumped, and she did not look at Elric as she began to guide her horse slowly down towards the sorcerer

of Pan Tang. Elric followed, conscious of his own in-
decision, yet half-careless of it. What did it matter to
him if . . . ?

The music began, faintly at first, but beginning to
swell with an attractive, poignant sweetness, evoking
nostalgic memories, offering peace and giving life a
sharp meaning, all at once. If the music came from
instruments, then they were not earthly. It produced
in him a yearning to turn about and discover its
source, but he resisted it. Yishana, on the other hand,
was evidently not finding the music so easily resisted.
She had wheeled completely round, her face radiant,
her lips trembling and tears shining in her eyes.

Elric, in his wanderings in unearthly realms, had
heard music like it before—it echoed many of the bizarre symphonies of old Melniboné—and it did not
draw him as it drew Yishana. He recognised swiftly
that she was in danger, and as she came past him,
spurring her horse, he reached out to grab her
bridle.

Her whip slashed at his hand and, cursing with
unexpected pain, he dropped the bridle. She went
past him, galloping up to the crest of the hill and
vanishing over it in an instant.

'Yishana!' He shouted at her desperately, but his
voice would not carry over the pulsing music. He
looked back, hoping that Theleb K'aarna would
lend help, but the sorcerer was riding rapidly away.
Evidently, on hearing the music, he had come to a
swift decision.

Elric raced after Yishana, screaming for her to
turn back. His own horse reached the top of the hill
and he saw her bent over her steed's neck as she
goaded it towards the shining citadel.

'Yishana! You go to your doom!'

Now she had reached the outer limits of the
citadel, and her horse's feet seemed to strike off

shimmering waves of colour as they touched the Chaos-disturbed ground surrounding the place. Although he knew it was too late to stop her, Elric continued to speed after her, hoping to reach her before she entered the citadel itself.

But, even as he entered the rainbow swirl, he saw what appeared to be a dozen Yishanas going through a dozen gateways into the citadel. Oddly refracted light created the illusion and made it impossible to tell which was the real Yishana.

With Yishana's disappearance the music stopped and Elric thought he heard a faint whisper of laughter following it. His horse was by this time becoming increasingly difficult to control, and he did not trust himself to it. He dismounted, his legs wreathed in radiant mist, and let the horse go. It galloped off, snorting its terror.

Elric's left hand moved to the hilt of his runesword, but he hesitated to draw it. Once pulled from its scabbard, the blade would demand souls before it allowed itself to be resheathed. Yet it was his only weapon. He withdrew his hand, and the blade seemed to quiver angrily at his side.

'Not yet, Stormbringer. There may be forces within who are stronger even than you!'

He began to wade through the faintly-resisting light swirls. He was half-blinded by the scintillating colours around him, which sometimes shone dark blue, silver, and red; sometimes gold, light green, amber. He also felt the sickening lack of any sort of orientation—distance, depth, breadth were meaningless. He recognised what he had only experienced in an astral form—the odd, timeless, spaceless quality that marked a Realm of the Higher Worlds.

He drifted, pushing his body in the direction in which he guessed Yishana had gone, for by now he had lost sight of the gateway or any of its mirage images.

He realised that, unless he was doomed to drift here until he starved, he must draw Stormbringer; for the runeblade could resist the influence of Chaos.

This time, when he gripped the sword's hilt, he felt a shock run up his arm and infuse his body with vitality. The sword came free from the scabbard. From the huge blade, carved with strange old runes, a black radiance poured, meeting the shifting colours of Chaos and dispersing them.

Now Elric shrieked the age-old battle-ululation of his folk and pressed on into the citadel, slashing at the intangible images that swirled on all sides. The gateway was ahead, and Elric knew it now, for his sword had shown him which were the mirages. It was open as Elric reached the portal. He paused for a moment, his lips moving as he remembered an invocation that he might need later. Arioch, Lord of Chaos, patron god-demon of his ancestors, was a negligent power and whimful—he could not rely on Arioch to aid him here, unless . . .

In slow graceful strides, a golden beast with eyes of ruby-fire was loping down the passage that led from the portal. Bright though the eyes were, they seemed blind, and its huge, doglike muzzle was closed. Yet its path could only lead it to Elric and, as it neared him, the mouth suddenly gaped showing coral fangs. In silence it came to a halt, the blind eyes never once settling on the albino, and then sprang!

Elric staggered back, raising the sword in defence. He was flung to the ground by the beast's weight and felt its body cover him. It was cold, cold, and it made no attempt to savage him—just lay on top of him and let the cold permeate his body.

Elric began to shiver as he pushed at the chilling body of the beast. Stormbringer moaned and mur-

mured in his hand, and then it pierced some part of
the beast's body, and a horrible cold strength began
to fill the albino. Reinforced by the beast's own life-
force, he heaved upwards. The beast continued to
smother him, though now a thin, barely audible
sound was coming from it. Elric guessed that
Stormbringer's small wound was hurting the creature.

Desperately, for he was shaking and aching with
cold, he moved the sword and stabbed again. Again
the thin sound from the beast; again cold energy
flooded through him, and again he heaved. This
time the beast was flung off and crawled back
towards the portal. Elric sprang up, raised Stormbringer high, and brought the sword down on the
golden creature's skull. The skull shattered as ice
might shatter.

Elric rang forward into the passage and, once
within, the place became filled with roars and
shrieks that echoed and were magnified. It was as if
the voice that the cold beast had lacked outside was
shouting its death-agonies here.

Now the floor rose until he was running up a spi-
ral ramp. Looking down, he shuddered, for he
looked into an infinite pit of subtle, dangerous
colours that swam about in such a way that he could
hardly take his eyes from them. He even felt his
body begin to leave the ramp and go towards the pit,
but he strengthened his grip on the sword and dis-
ciplined himself to climb on.

Upwards, as he looked, was the same as downwards. Only the ramp had any kind of constancy,
and this began to take on the appearance of a thinly-
cut jewel, through which he could see the pit and in
which it was reflected.

Greens and blues and yellows predominated, but
there were also traces of dark red, black, and orange,

and many other colours not in an ordinary human spectrum.

Elric knew he was in some province of the Higher Worlds and guessed that it would not be long before the ramp led him to new danger.

Danger did not seem to await him when at last he came to the end of the ramp and stepped on to a bridge of similar stuff, which led over the scintillating pit to an archway that shone with a steady blue light.

He crossed the bridge cautiously and as cautiously entered the arch. Everything was blue-tinged here, even himself; and he trod on, the blue becoming deeper and deeper as he progressed.

Then Stormbringer began to murmur and, either warned by the sword or by some sixth sense of his own, Elric wheeled to his right. Another archway had appeared there and from this there began to shine a light as deep red as the other was blue. Where the two met was a purple of fantastic richness and Elric stared at this, experiencing a similar hypnotic pull as he had had when climbing the ramp. Again his mind was stronger, and he forced himself to enter the red arch. At once another arch appeared to his left, sending a beam of green light to merge with the red, and another to his left brought yellow light, one ahead brought mauve until he seemed trapped within the criss-cross of beams. He slashed at them with Stormbringer, and the black radiance reduced the beams for a moment to streamers of light, which reformed again. Elric continued to move forward.

Now, looming through the confusion of colour, a shape appeared and Elric thought it was that of a man.

Man it was in shape—but not in size it seemed. Yet, when it drew closer, it was no giant—less than

Elric's height. Still it gave the *impression* of vast proportions, rather as if it *were* a giant and Elric had grown to its size.

It blundered towards Elric and went *through* him. It was not that the man was intangible—it was Elric who felt the ghost. The creature's mass seemed of incredible density. The creature was turning, its huge hands reaching out, its face a mocking grimace. Elric struck at it with Strombringer and was astonished as the runesword was halted, making no impression on the creature's bulk.

Yet when it grasped Elric, its hands went through him. Elric backed away, grinning now in relief. Then he saw with some terror that the light was gleaming through him. He had been right—*he* was the ghost!

The creature reached out for him again, grabbed him again, failed to hold him.

Elric, conscious that he was in no physical danger from the monster, yet also highly conscious that his sanity was about to be permanently impaired, turned and fled.

Quite suddenly he was in a hall, the walls of which were of the same unstable, shifting colours as the rest of the place. But sitting on a stool in the centre of the hall, holding in his hands some tiny creatures that seemed to be running about on his palm, was a small figure who looked up at Elric and grinned merrily.

'Welcome, King of Melniboné. And how fares the last ruler of my favourite earthly race?'

The figure was dressed in shimmering motley. On his head was a tall, spiked crown—a travesty of and a comment upon the crowns of the mighty. His face was angular and his mouth wide.

'Greetings, Lord Balo,' Elric made a mock bow. 'Strange hospitality you offer in your welcome.'

'Ahaha—it did not amuse you, eh? Men are so much harder to please than gods—you would not think it, would you?'

'Men's pleasures are rarely so elaborate. Where is Queen Yishana?'

'Allow me my pleasures also, mortal. Here she is, I think.' Balo plucked at one of the tiny creatures on his palm. Elric stepped forward and saw that Yishana was indeed there, as were many of the lost soldiers. Balo looked up at him and winked. 'They are so much easier to handle in this size.'

'I do not doubt it, though I wonder if it is not we who are larger rather than they who are smaller....'

'You are astute, mortal. But can you guess how this came to be?'

'Your creature back there—your pits and colours and archways—somehow they warp—what?'

'*Mass*, King Elric. But you would not understand such concepts. Even the Lords of Melniboné, most godlike and intelligent of mortals, only learned how to manipulate the elements in ritual, invocation, and spell, but never understood what they manipulated—that is where the Lords of the Higher Worlds score, whatever their differences.'

'But I survived without need for spells. I survived by disciplining my mind!'

'That helped, for certain—but you forget your greatest asset—that disturbing blade there. You use it in your petty problems to aid you, and you never realise that it is like making use of a mighty war galley to catch a sprat. That sword represents power in *any* Realm, King Elric!'

'Aye, so it might. This does not interest me. Why are you here, Lord Balo?'

Balo chuckled, his laughter rich and musical. 'Oho, I am in disgrace. I quarrelled with my masters, who took exception to a joke of mine about their insignificance and egotism, about their destiny and their pride. Bad taste to them, King, is any hint of their own oblivion. I made a joke in bad taste. I fled from the Higher Worlds to Earth, where, unless invoked, the Lords of Law or Chaos can rarely interfere. You will like my intention, Elric, as would any Melnibonéan—I intend to establish my own Realm on Earth—the Realm of Paradox. A little from Law, a little from Chaos—a Realm of opposites, of curiosities and jokes.'

'I'm thinking we already have such a world as you describe, Lord Balo, with no need for you to create it!'

'Earnest irony, King Elric, for an insouciant man of Melniboné.'

'Ah, that it may be. I am a boor on occasions such as these. Will you release Yishana and myself?'

'But you and I are giants—I have given you the status and appearance of a god. You and I could be partners in this enterprise of mine!'

'Unfortunately, Lord Balo, I do not possess your range of humour and am unfitted for such an exalted role. Besides,' Elric grinned suddenly, 'it is in my mind that the Lords of the Higher Worlds will not easily let drop the matter of your ambition, since it appears to conflict so strongly with theirs.'

Balo laughed but said nothing.

Elric also smiled, but it was an attempt to hide his racing thoughts. 'What do you intend to do if I refuse?'

'Why, Elric, you would not refuse! I can think of many subtle pranks that I could play on you . . .'

'Indeed? And the Black Swords?'

'Ah, yes . . .'

'Balo, in your mirth and obsessions you have not considered everything thoroughly. You should have exerted more effort to vanquish me before I came here.'

Now Elric's eyes gleamed hot and he lifted the sword, crying:

'*Arioch! Master! I invoke thee, Lord of Chaos!*'

Balo started. 'Cease that, King Elric!'

'*Arioch—here is a soul for you to claim!*'

'Quiet, I say!'

'*Arioch! Hear me!*' Elric's voice was loud and desperate.

Balo let his tiny playthings fall and rose hurriedly, skipping towards Elric.

'Your invocation is unheeded!' He laughed, reaching out for Elric. But Stormbringer moaned and shuddered in Elric's hand and Balo withdrew his hand. His face became serious and frowning.

'*Arioch of the Seven Darks—your servant calls you!*'

The walls of flame trembled and began to fade. Balo's eyes widened and jerked this way and that.

'*Oh, Lord Arioch—come reclaim your straying Balo!*'

'You cannot!' Balo scampered across the room where one section of the flame had faded entirely, revealing darkness beyond.

'Sadly for you, little jester, he can . . .' The voice was sardonic and yet beautiful. From the darkness stepped a tall figure, no longer the shapeless gibbering thing that had, until now, been Arioch's favoured manifestation when visiting the Realm of Earth. Yet the great beauty of the newcomer, filled as it was with a kind of compassion mingled with pride, cruelty, and sadness, showed at once that he could not be human. He was clad in doublet of pulsing scarlet, hose of ever-changing hue, a long golden sword at his hips. His eyes were large, but slanted high, his hair was long and as golden as the sword, his lips were full and his chin pointed like his ears.

'Arioch!' Balo stumbled backwards as the Lord of Chaos advanced.

'It was your mistake, Balo,' Elric said from behind the jester. 'Did you not realise only the Kings of Melniboné may invoke Arioch and bring him to the Realm of Earth? It has been their age-old privilege.'

'And much have they abused it,' said Arioch, smiling faintly as Balo grovelled. 'However, this service you have done us, Elric, will make up for past misuses. I was not amused by the matter of the Mist Giant . . .'

Even Elric was awed by the incredibly powerful presence of the Chaos Lord. He also felt much relieved, for he had not been sure that Arioch could be summoned in this way.

Now Arioch stretched an arm down towards Balo and lifted the jester by his collar so that he jerked and struggled in the air, his face writhing in fear and consternation.

Arioch took hold of Balo's head and squeezed it. Elric looked on in amazement as the head began to shrink. Arioch took Balo's legs and bent them in, folding Balo up and kneading him in his slender, inhuman hands until he was a small, solid ball. Arioch then popped the ball into his mouth and swallowed it.

'I have not eaten him, Elric,' he said with another faint smile. 'It is merely the easiest way of transporting him back to the Realms from which he came. He has transgressed and will be punished. All this'— he waved an arm to indicate the citadel—'is unfortunate and contradicts the plans we of Chaos have for Earth—plans which will involve you, our servant, and make you mighty.'

Elric bowed to his master. 'I am honoured, Lord Arioch, though I seek no favours.'

Arioch's silvery voice lost some of its beauty and his face seemed to cloud for a second. 'You are pledged to serve Chaos, Elric, as were your ancestors. You *will* serve Chaos! The time draws near when both Law and Chaos will battle for the Realm of Earth—and Chaos shall win! Earth will be incorporated into our Realm and you will join the hierarchy of Chaos, become immortal as we are!'

'Immortality offers little to me, my lord.'

'Ah, Elric, have the men of Melniboné become as the half-apes who now dominate Earth with their puny "civilisations"? Are you no better than these Young Kingdom upstarts? Think what we offer!'

'I shall, my lord, when the time you mention comes.' Elric's head was still lowered.

'You shall indeed,' Arioch raised his arms. 'Now to transport this toy of Balo's to its proper Realm, and redress the trouble he has caused, lest some hint reaches our opponents before the proper time.'

Arioch's voice swelled like the singing of a million brazen bells and Elric sheathed his sword and clapped his hands over his ears to stop the pain.

Then Elric felt his body seem to *shred* apart, swell and stretch until it became like smoke drifting on air. Then, faster, the smoke began to be drawn together, becoming denser and denser and he seemed to be shrinking now. All around him were rolling banks of colour, flashes and indescribable noises. Then came a vast blackness and he closed his eyes against the images that seemed reflected in the blackness.

When he opened them he stood in the valley and the singing citadel was gone. Only Yishana and a few surprised-looking soldiers stood there. Yishana ran towards him.

'Elric—was it you who saved us?'

'I must claim only part of the credit,' he said.

'Not all my soldiers are here,' she said, inspecting the men. Where are the rest—and the villagers abducted earlier?'

'If Balo's tastes are like his masters', then I fear they now have the honour of being part of a demigod. The Lords of Chaos are not flesh-eaters, of course, being of the Higher Worlds, but there is something they savour in men which satisfies them . . .'

Yishana hugged her body as if in cold. 'He was huge—I cannot believe that his citadel could contain his bulk!'

'The citadel was more than a dwelling-place, that was obvious. Somehow it changed size, shape—and other things I cannot describe. Arioch of Chaos transported it and Balo back to where they belong.'

'Arioch! But he is one of the Greatest Six! How did he come to Earth?'

'An old pact with my remote ancestors. By calling him they allow him to spend a short time in our realm, and he repays them with some favour. This was done.'

'Come, Elric,' she took his arm. 'Let's away from the valley.'

Elric was weak and enfeebled by the efforts of summoning Arioch, and the experiences he had had before and since the episode. He could hardly walk; and soon it was Yishana who supported him as they made slow progress, the dazed warriors following in their wake, towards the nearest village, where they could obtain rest and horses to take them back to Dhakos.

FIVE

~~~~~~~~~~~~~~~~~

As they staggered past the blasted ruins of Thokara, Yishana pointed suddenly at the sky.

'What is that?'

A great shape was winging its way towards them. It had the appearance of a butterfly, but a butterfly with wings so huge they blotted out the sun.

'Can it be some creature of Balo's left behind?' she speculated.

'Hardly likely,' he replied. 'This has the appearance of a monster conjured by a human sorcerer.'

'Theleb K'aarna!'

'He has surpassed himself,' Elric said wryly. 'I did not think him capable.'

'It is his vengeance on us, Elric!'

'That seems reasonable. But I am weak, Yishana—and Stormbringer needs souls if it is to replenish my strength.' He turned a calculating eye on the warriors behind him who were gaping up at the creature as it came nearer. Now they could see it had a man's body, covered with hairs or feathers hued like a peacock's.

The air whistled as it descended, its fifty-foot wings dwarfing the seven feet of head and body. From its head grew two curling horns, and its arms terminated in long talons.

'We are doomed, Elric!' cried Yishana. She saw that the warriors were fleeing and she cried after them to come back. Elric stood there passively, knowing that alone he could not defeat the butter-fly-creature.

'Best go with them, Yishana,' he murmured. 'I think it will be satisfied with me.'

'No!'

He ignored her and stepped towards the creature as it landed and began to glide over the ground in his direction. He drew a quiescent Stormbringer, which felt heavy in his hand. A little strength flowed into him, but not enough. His only hope was to strike a good blow at the creature's vitals and draw some of its own life-force into himself.

The creature's voice shrilled at him, and the strange, insane face twisted as he approached. Elric realised that this was no true supernatural denizen of the nether worlds, but a once-human creature warped by Theleb K'aarna's sorcery. At least it was mortal, and he had only physical strength to contend with. In better condition it would have been easy for him—but now ...

The wings beat at the air as the taloned hands grasped at him. He took Stormbringer in both hands and swung the runeblade at the thing's neck. Swiftly the wings folded in to protect its neck and Storm-bringer became entangled in the strange, sticky flesh. A talon caught Elric's arm, ripping it to the bone. He yelled in pain and yanked the sword from the en-folding wing.

He tried to steady himself for another blow, but the monster grabbed his wounded arm and began drawing him towards its now lowered head—and the horns that curled from it.

He struggled, hacking at the thing's arms with the extra strength that came with the threat of death.

Then he heard a cry from behind him and saw a figure from the corner of his eye, a figure that leapt

forward with two blades gleaming in either hand.
The swords slashed at the talons and with a shriek
the creature turned on Elric's would-be rescuer.

It was Moonglum. Elric fell backwards, breathing
hard, as he watched his little red-headed friend en-
gage the monster.

But Moonglum would not survive for long, unless
aided.

Elric racked his brain for some spell that would
help; but he was too weak, even if he could think of
one, to raise the energy necessary to summon supernatural help.

And then it came to him! Yishana! She was not as
exhausted as he. But could she do it?

He turned as the air moaned to the beating of the
creature's wings. Moonglum was only just managing
to hold it off, his two swords flashing rapidly as he
parried every effort to grasp him.

'Yishana!' croaked the albino.

She came up to him and placed a hand on his. 'We
could leave, Elric—perhaps hide from that thing.'

'No. I must help Moonglum. Listen—you realise
how desperate our position is, do you not? Then
keep that in mind while you recite this rune with
me. Perhaps together we may succeed. There are
many kinds of lizards in these parts, are there not?'

'Aye—many.'

'Then this is what you must say—and remember
that we shall all perish by Theleb K'aarna's servant
if you are not successful.'

In the half worlds, where dwelt the master-types
of all creatures other than Man, an entity stirred,
hearing its name. The entity was called Haaashaastaak; and it was scaly and cold, with no true intellect,
such as men and gods possessed, but an *awareness*,
which served it as well if not better. It was brother,

on this plane, to such entities as Meerclar, Lord of the Cats, Roofdrak, Lord of the Dogs, Nuru-ah, Lord of the Cattle, and many, many others. This was Haaashaastaak, Lord of the Lizards. It did not really hear words in the exact sense, but it heard rhythms which meant much to it, even though it did not know why. The rhythms were being repeated over and over again, but seemed too faint to be worth much attention. It stirred and yawned, but did nothing . . .

> '*Haaashaastaak, Lord of Lizards,*
> *Your children were fathers of men,*
> *Haaashaastaak, Prince of Reptiles.*
> *Come aid a grandchild now!*
>
> '*Haaashaastaak, Father of Scales,*
> *Cold-blooded bringer of life . . .*'

It was a bizarre scene, with Elric and Yishana desperately chanting the rune over and over again as Moonglum fought on, slowly losing strength.

Haaashaastaak quivered and became more curious. The rhythms were no stronger, yet they seemed more insistent. He would travel, he decided, to that place where those he watched over dwelt. He knew that if he answered the rhythms, he would have to obey whatever source they had. He was not, of course, aware that such decisions had been implanted into him in a far distant age—the time before the creation of Earth, when the Lords of Law and Chaos, then inhabitants of a single realm and known by another name, had watched over the forming of things and laid down the manner and logic in which things should behave, following their great edict from the voice of the Cosmic Balance—the voice which had never spoken since.

Haaashaastaak betook himself, a little slothfully, to Earth.

Elric and Yishana were still chanting hoarsely, as Haaashaastaak made his sudden appearance. He had the look of a huge iguana, and his eyes were many-coloured, many faceted jewels, his scales seeming of gold, silver, and other rich metals. A slightly hazy outline surrounded him, as if he had brought part of his own environment with him.

Yishana gasped and Elric breathed a deep sigh. As a child he had learned the languages of all animal-masters, and now he must recall the simple language of the lizard-master, Haaashaastaak.

His need fired his brain, and the words came suddenly.

'*Haaashaastaak*,' he cried pointing at the butterfly-creature, '*mokik ankkuh!*'

The lizard lord turned its jewelled eyes on the creature and its great tongue suddenly shot out towards it, curling around the monster. It shrilled in terror as it was drawn towards the lizard lord's great maw. Legs and arms kicked as the mouth closed on it. Several gulps and Haaashaastaak had swallowed Theleb K'aarna's prize creation. Then it turned its head uncertainly about for a few moments and vanished.

Pain began to throb now through Elric's torn arm as Moonglum staggered towards him, grinning in relief.

'I followed behind you at a distance as you requested,' he said, 'since you suspected treachery from Theleb K'aarna. But than I spied the sorcerer coming this way and followed him to a cave in yonder hills,' he pointed. 'But when the deceased,' he laughed shakily, 'emerged from the cave, I decided that it would be best to chase *that*, for I had the feeling it was going in your direction.'

'I am glad you were so astute,' Elric said.

'It was your doing, really,' Moonglum replied. 'For, if you hadn't anticipated treachery from Theleb K'aarna, I might not have been here at the right moment.' Moonglum suddenly sank to the grass, leaned back, grinned, and fainted.

Elric felt very dazed himself. 'I do not think we need fear anything more from your sorcerer just yet, Yishana,' he said. 'Let us rest here and refresh ourselves. Perhaps then your cowardly soldiers will have returned, and we can send them to a village to get us some horses.'

They stretched out on the grass and, lying in each other's arms, went to sleep.

Elric was astonished to wake in a bed, a soft bed. He opened his eyes and saw Yishana and Moonglum smiling down at him.

'How long have I been here?'

'More than two days. You did not wake when the horses came, so we had the warriors construct a stretcher to bear you to Dhakos. You are in my palace.'

Elric cautiously moved his stiff, bandaged arm. It was still painful. 'Are my belongings still at the inn?'

'Perhaps, if they have not been stolen. Why?'

'I have a pouch of herbs there, which will heal this arm quickly and also supply me with a little strength, which I need badly.'

'I will go and see if they are still there,' Moonglum said and walked from the chamber.

Yishana stroked Elric's milk-white hair. 'I have much to thank you for, wolf,' said she. 'You have saved my kingdom—perhaps all the Young Kingdoms. In my eyes you are redeemed for my brother's death.'

'Oh, I thank you, madam,' said Elric with a mocking tone.

She laughed. 'You are still a Melnibonéan.'

'Still that, aye.'

'A strange mixture, however. Sensitive and cruel, sardonic and loyal to your little friend Moonglum. I look forward to knowing you better, my lord.'

'As to that, I am not sure if you will have the opportunity.'

She gave him a hard look. 'Why?'

'Your résumé of my character was incomplete, Queen Yishana—you should have added "careless of the world—and yet vengeful." I wish to be revenged on your pet wizard.'

'But he is spent, surely—you said so yourself.'

'I am, as you remarked, still a Melnibonéan! My arrogant blood calls vengeance on an upstart!'

'Forget Theleb K'aarna. I will have him hunted by my White Leopards. Even his sorcery will not win against such savages as they are!'

'Forget him? Oh, no!'

'Elric, Elric—I will give you my kingdom, declare you ruler of Jharkor, if you will let me be your consort.'

He reached out and stroked her bare arm with his good hand.

'You are unrealistic, queen. To take such an action would bring wholesale rebellion in your land. To your folk, I am still the Traitor of Imrryr.'

'Not now—now you are the Hero of Jharkor.'

'How so? They did not know of their peril and thus will feel no gratitude. It were best that I settled my debt with your wizard and went on my way. The streets must already be full of rumours that you have taken your brother's murderer to your bed. Your popularity with your subjects must be at its lowest, madam.'

'I do not care.'

'You will if your nobles lead the people in insurrection and crucify you naked in the city square.'

'You are familiar with our customs.'

'We Melnibonéans are a learned folk, queen.'

'Well versed in all the arts.'

'All of them.' Again he felt his blood race as she rose and barred the door. At that moment he felt no need for the herbs which Moonglum had gone to find.

When he tiptoed from the room that night, he found Moonglum waiting patiently in the antechamber. Moonglum proffered the pouch with a wink. But Elric's mood was not light. He took bunches of herbs from the pouch and selected what he needed.

Moonglum grimaced as he watched Elric chew and swallow the stuff. Then together they stole from the palace.

Armed with Stormbringer and mounted, Elric rode slightly behind his friend as Moonglum led the way towards the hills beyond Dhakos.

'If I know the sorcerers of Pan Tang,' murmured the albino, 'then Theleb K'aarna will be more exhausted than was I. With luck we will come upon him sleeping.'

'I shall wait outside the cave in that case,' said Moonglum, for he now had some experience of Elric's vengeance-taking and did not relish watching Theleb K'aarna's slow death.

They galloped speedily until the hills were reached and Moonglum showed Elric the cave mouth.

Leaving his horse, the albino went soft-footed into the cave, his runesword ready.

Moonglum waited nervously for Theleb K'aarna's first shrieks, but none came. He waited until dawn began to bring the first faint light and then Elric, face frozen with anger emerged from the cave.

Savagely he grasped his horse's reins and swung himself into the saddle.

'Are you satisfied?' Moonglum asked tentatively.

'Satisfied, no! The dog has vanished!'

'Gone—but ...'

'He was more cunning than I thought. There are several caves and I sought him in all of them. In the farthest I discovered traces of sorcerous runes on the walls and floor. He has transported himself somewhere and I could not discover where, in spite of deciphering most of the runes! Perhaps he went to Pan Tang.'

'Ah, then our quest has been futile. Let us return to Dhakos and enjoy a little more of Yishana's hospitality.'

'No—we go to Pan Tang.'

'But, Elric, Theleb K'aarna's brother sorcerers dwell there in strength; and Jagreen Lern, the theocrat, forbids visitors!'

'No matter. I wish to finish my business with Theleb K'aarna.'

'You have no proof that he is there!'

'*No matter!*'

And then Elric was spurring his horse away, riding like a man possessed or fleeing from dreadful peril—and perhaps he was both possessed and fleeing. Moonglum did not follow at once but thoughtfully watched his friend gallop off. Not normally introspective, he wondered if Yishana had perhaps affected the albino more strongly than he would have wished. He did not think that vengeance on Theleb K'aarna was Elric's prime desire in refusing to return to Dhakos.

Then he shrugged and clapped his heels to his steed's flanks, racing to catch up with Elric as the cold dawn rose, wondering if they would continue towards Pan Tang once Dhakos was far enough behind.

But Elric's head contained no thoughts, only emotion flooded him—emotion he did not wish to analyse. His white hair streaming behind him, his dead-white, handsome face set, his slender hands tightly clutching the stallion's reins, he rode. And only his strange, crimson eyes reflected the misery and conflict within him.

In Dhakos that morning, other eyes held misery, but not for too long. Yishana was a pragmatic queen.

Fantasy from Ace
fanciful and fantastic!

☐ 39621-0 **JOURNEY TO APRILIOTH** $2.50
Eileen Kernaghan

☐ 15313-5 **THE DOOR IN THE HEDGE** $2.25
Robin McKinley

☐ 47073-4 **THE LAST CASTLE** $1.95
Jack Vance

☐ 14295-8 **THE DEVIL IN THE FOREST** $2.25
Gene Wolfe

☐ 10253-0 **CHANGELING** $2.95
Roger Zelazny

☐ 20403-1 **ELSEWHERE Vol. I** $2.75
Terri Windling and Mark Alan Arnold (eds.)

☐ 20404-X **ELSEWHERE Vol. II** $2.95
Terri Windling and Mark Alan Arnold (eds.)

Available wherever paperbacks are sold or use this coupon.

ACE SCIENCE FICTION
Book Mailing Service
P.O. Box 690, Rockville Centre, NY 11571

Please send me the titles checked above. I enclose _____.
Include $1.00 for postage and handling if one book is ordered; 50¢ per book for
two or more. California, Illinois, New York and Tennessee residents please add
sales tax.

NAME _____

ADDRESS _____

CITY _____ STATE/ZIP _____

(allow six weeks for delivery)

SF 1